It Was Her Wedding Day.

It was the day her oldest, most cherished dream was coming true.

Ellie wanted to be ready. She wanted to be perfect for this perfect man whom she had adored from the moment she could say his name. *Lee*.

She walked to the closet and the carefully preserved wedding gown that awaited her. It was a dress made for a princess. Antique lace and virginal white satin hung in luxurious folds from a padded hanger.

"How pretty you must have looked in this dress, Momma," she whispered. "How Daddy must have loved you."

Just as Lee would grow to love *her*.

She knew that he would. In time. Once he got to know her better. Once he understood that she was a woman, not a child....

Dear Reader,

Welcome to Silhouette Desire, where you can indulge yourself every month with six passionate, powerful and provocative romances! And you can take romance one step further.... Look inside for details about our exciting new contest, "Silhouette Makes You a Star."

Popular author Mary Lynn Baxter returns to Desire with our MAN OF THE MONTH when *The Millionaire Comes Home* to Texas to reunite with the woman he could never forget. Rising star Sheri WhiteFeather's latest story features a *Comanche Vow* that leads to a marriage of convenience...until passionate love transforms it into the real thing.

It's our pleasure to present you with a new miniseries entitled 20 AMBER COURT, featuring four twentysomething female friends who share an address...and their discoveries about life and love. Don't miss the launch title, *When Jayne Met Erik,* by beloved author Elizabeth Bevarly. The scandalous Desire miniseries FORTUNES OF TEXAS: THE LOST HEIRS continues with *Fortune's Secret Daughter* by Barbara McCauley. Alexandra Sellers offers you another sumptuous story in her miniseries SONS OF THE DESERT: THE SULTANS, *Sleeping with the Sultan.* And the talented Cindy Gerard brings you a touching love story about a man of honor pledged to marry an innocent young woman with a secret, in *The Bridal Arrangement.*

Treat yourself to all six of these tantalizing tales from Silhouette Desire.

Enjoy!

Joan Marlow Golan

Joan Marlow Golan
Senior Editor, Silhouette Desire

Please address questions and book requests to:
Silhouette Reader Service
U.S.: 3010 Walden Ave., P.O. Box 1325, Buffalo, NY 14269
Canadian: P.O. Box 609, Fort Erie, Ont. L2A 5X3

The Bridal Arrangement

CINDY GERARD

Published by Silhouette Books

America's Publisher of Contemporary Romance

This book is dedicated to those who understand that courage is often silent and proud.

My thanks to Joan Marlow Golan for her vision and trust, to Carole Loveless for sharing and as always, to Glenna McReynolds, for her brilliant insight, generosity and friendship.

 SILHOUETTE BOOKS

ISBN 0-373-76392-1

THE BRIDAL ARRANGEMENT

Copyright © 2001 by Cindy Gerard

Visit Silhouette at www.eHarlequin.com

Printed in U.S.A.

Books by Cindy Gerard

Silhouette Desire

The Cowboy Takes a Lady #957
Lucas: The Loner #975
*The Bride Wore Blue #1012
*A Bride for Abel Greene #1052
*A Bride for Crimson Falls #1076
†*The Outlaw's Wife* #1175
†*Marriage, Outlaw Style* #1185
†*The Outlaw Jesse James* #1198
Lone Star Prince #1256
In His Loving Arms #1293
Lone Star Knight #1353
The Bridal Arrangement #1392

*Northern Lights Brides
†Outlaw Hearts

CINDY GERARD

If asked, "What's your idea of heaven?" Cindy Gerard would say a warm sun, a cool breeze, pan pizza and a good book. If she had to settle for one of the four, she'd opt for the book, with the pizza running a close second. Inspired by the pleasure she's received from the books she's read and her longtime love affair with her husband, Tom, Cindy now creates her own evocative and sensual love stories about compelling characters and complex relationships.

This number-one bestselling author of close to twenty books has received numerous industry awards, among them the National Readers' Choice Award, multiple *Romantic Times Magazine* nominations and two RITA Award nominations from the Romance Writers of America. Cindy loves to hear from her readers and invites them to visit her web page at www.TLT.com/authors/cgerard.httm.

SILHOUETTE MAKES YOU A STAR!
Feel like a star with Silhouette.
Look for the exciting details of our new contest
inside all of these fabulous Silhouette novels:

One

Lee Savage felt like a man on a collision course with disaster. Guilt settled, heavy and solid as he climbed out of his pickup, thumbed back his Stetson and worked to ignore the sad condition of Shiloh Ranch. Even the dark tint of his sunglasses couldn't dim the ragged edges of neglect.

Every building and fence within eyesight needed painting or repair. A pair of black shutters, faded to a chalky gray, hung crookedly from a broken hinge on the second story of the house. And those were just surface blemishes. Still, it all registered on a peripheral level as he climbed the front porch steps and a rotted floorboard creaked beneath his booted foot.

With a resolute set of his jaw, he squared his shoulders and shut out everything but the job he'd come to do. He raised his hand, made a fist and knocked on the door of the only real home he'd ever known.

Only moments passed before small, delicate fingers brushed aside an age-yellowed lace curtain and a pair of soft violet eyes peered out at him from behind the wavy windowpane.

He knew those eyes, but he knew them as a child's eyes. At nineteen, it seemed that Ellie Shiloh was hardly more than a child now. Yet, as the door flew open and she slipped outside, he recognized both an ageless knowledge and an endless innocence in their sparkling, velvet depths.

Involuntarily he felt his mouth soften with tenderness as she tugged the door shut behind her. The scent of cinnamon and vanilla and a sweetly musky fragrance he couldn't quite identify wafted lightly in her wake, stirring rich reminders of home—along with unsettling twinges of awareness.

"Hello, Ellie," he managed in a rusty voice, swamped by memories of sugar cookies cooling on a baking rack, stunned by more immediate sensory impressions of silken skin and sensual, probing eyes— eyes completing a smile that was too huge and too hopeful and unreasonably happy under the circumstances.

"Mornin', Lee." Her voice was as pure and perfect as the Montana air. "And what a fine morning."

Tugging the belt of her fussy pink robe tighter around her tiny waist, she tipped her face toward the golden glow of the horizon. She drew in a deep, pleasured breath, then tilted her head, giving him a playful, assessing once-over. "A little early for someone of your advanced years to be up and around, though, isn't it?"

She was messing with him. He'd been eighteen when he'd left Shiloh, and he'd rarely made it back in the fifteen years since. When he had, she'd always liked to tease him about being older and wiser...practically ancient in the face of her youth. Not only couldn't he smile at her gentle barb as he once might have, it took effort to keep from cringing. He notched his chin instead and stared past a truth he couldn't ignore—and beyond an unnerving notion that the laughter bubbling in her eyes was prodded as much by blissful ignorance as it was by mischief.

She had no idea. No idea at all, what she was getting in to. The fact that she found humor instead of uncertainty in the situation proved it—though it didn't change what had to be done.

He tugged off his sunglasses, folded them into the breast pocket of his shirt and transferred his attention toward his polished boot tips, only to be thrown off balance again. Damn if his heart didn't catch—just a little half hitch—at the sight of the tiny pink toes peeking out from beneath her floor-length flowing robe.

He cleared his throat. Got down to business. "So. The fourteenth will work out for you, then?"

He could sense the softness of her gaze even before he lifted his head, struggling with his bad feelings about all of this.

Her nod was quick and certain. "Oh, yes, the fourteenth is perfect. I've ordered sunshine. And a sweet breeze. It only seems right, don't you think?"

He studied her gamine features—the saucily turned-up nose, delicately winged brows, tiny fairy ears partially hidden beneath a silken fall of riotously tangled copper and gold curls that tumbled midway down her back. She looked as though she ought to be running barefoot through a sun-dappled forest, flower

petals woven in her hair, hummingbirds and butter-
flies flitting around her head as she conjured up her
sunshine and her sweet breezes.

"Would that be all right, Lee?" he heard her ask
and knew he'd been so immersed in the daydream the
sight of her invoked that he must have missed something.

He shook his head, glanced toward the porch over-
hang where the spring breeze set a glass and copper
wind chime singing. On a deep breath, he met her
eyes again. "I'm sorry, Ellie. Would what be all
right?"

Her small hand reached out, touched his arm with
gentle care, as if she was suddenly in charge of looking out for him—him, who, at six foot two and 210,
towered over her by a full foot and outweighed her
by a good hundred pounds.

"Are you okay?" Her too-perfect brows were knit
together in studied concern.

"I'm fine," he grumbled abruptly, then made a
concentrated effort to relax as he pulled away from
the warm, tingling sensation that flowed along his arm
where her fingers had lingered with the lightness of
air.

Forcing a patience that neither fitted his dark mood
nor eased his tension, he softened his tone. "I'm fine,
Ellie. Now what was it that you asked me?"

"The church?" That beatific smile lit her face
again. "I'd like for it to be in the church, if it…if it
isn't too much trouble."

Her voice was as soft as meadow grass. Like her
eyes. Like her sweet, curvy little body bundled in that
fussy pink robe that he had no business thinking
about. That he hadn't stopped thinking about since

she'd breezed out into the morning to compete with the spring sunshine.

He made himself concentrate. She wanted a church. It was the first direct request she'd voiced since this whole sorry business started.

He gave her a clipped nod and bucked a sudden and unreasonable need to call the whole thing off. "Not a problem," he said instead, because he really had no choice. "I'll take care of it."

He didn't want to catalog the effect of yet another one of her radiant smiles. He didn't want to acknowledge how innocent, how trusting she looked. How unrelentingly bewitching.

Bewitching. Well. There was someplace he definitely didn't need to go. What he had to think about was duty. His. And a debt owed. A debt he had every intention of repaying as soon as he tidied up some unfinished business back in Texas.

"If you're sure you'll be okay, I'll be taking off then. I'll see you in two weeks."

He hadn't meant to sound so stiff and formal, but there it was, and there was nothing to be done for it now. He turned his back on those velvet eyes that pinned him with so much hope. Hope, when in fact, the situation seemed pretty hopeless at this point. Nothing to be done for that, either. Not at this late date.

He dug out his sunglasses, slipped them on and headed for his truck. He stopped abruptly, squinted against the burning ball of the morning sun and cupped the back of his neck where he swore he felt a sudden and soothing sensation of a caress.

She was watching him. He knew it. Just like he

knew it was a bad idea to turn around. He did it, anyway.

She'd walked to the edge of the porch. The bare toes of those impossibly tiny feet were curled against the morning chill; one arm hugged a porch post. With a china-doll cheek pressed against the peeling wood, she smiled with a shimmering expectancy that made his mouth go dry.

He drew in a bracing breath. "Everything's going to be fine, okay?"

She nodded, her eyes trying to make him believe it. The best thing for both of them was that he did. He didn't like the idea of leaving her on her own—even though he'd arranged for the neighbors to look in on her—and even if it was only for a couple of weeks while he tidied up those loose ends.

"I'll pick you up around ten on the fourteenth then," he croaked around the lump that had somehow found its way to his throat.

"Ten would be wonderful. Ten would be superb!" Her smile was far too buoyant for her to have yet grasped how drastically her life was about to change. "If…if it's not too much bother, that is," she added quietly.

Not too much bother? If the situation weren't dead serious, he'd laugh out loud. Hell. Picking her up and taking her to town was the least of the things that was bothering him.

For her sake he forced the requisite response. "You call now if you need anything. You've got my number, right?"

When she nodded, he headed back down the path toward his truck.

"Lee."

It took a long stride for him to stop, stiffen, react too strongly to the sound of his name on her petal-soft voice. He turned slowly—and found her shy smile touching.

''Thank you.'' A wealth of pride and far too much happiness colored her appreciation.

He merely nodded, knowing she was thanking him today for what would happen in two weeks that would change both of their lives forever.

In a church, he reminded himself when the sinking sensation that *he* was about to make the biggest mistake of *her* life, coupled with the realization that he still needed to pick up a wedding ring.

Ellie stood in the sun-drenched light of her east bedroom window. Excitement bubbled just beneath her skin like water dancing along a pebble-strewn brook.

She hugged her arms to her chest, bursting with feelings too big to contain. It was her wedding day. It was the day her oldest, most cherished dream was coming true.

Outside her window birdsong floated on a crisp breeze, a joyous harbinger of what was about to happen. In less than an hour Lee would be here.

He'd called her last night from the Sundown Hotel where he'd spent the night. She'd nearly melted at the sound of his voice. And she'd pictured him there—lying on the bed, his long legs crossed at the ankles, that deep frown that she found both endearing and sad creasing his brows. His dark hair would be a little mussed, his blue eyes would be crinkled with concern, with worry, and with the fatigue of his long drive from Houston—and, she hoped, with a little of the sweet anticipation she was feeling.

"And he's on his way to pick you up this very minute," she reminded herself, and felt another fluttering ripple of excitement.

She wanted to be ready. She wanted to be perfect for this perfect man that she had adored from the moment she could say his name.

She'd hurried through her morning chores—feeding the horses, gathering eggs—then given in to the luxury of a long, soaking bubble bath. And now she would get ready for her bridegroom.

Heart racing, she flew back to the full-length pedestal mirror in the corner of the room—the room she would soon share with Lee as his wife.

A flush crept from her cheeks to her throat and spread downward to stain the gentle round of her breasts revealed above the lacy white cups of the exquisite bra that had arrived just yesterday in the mail. She touched her fingers to sheer silk and delicate lace, blushed anew at the way her nipples hardened and pressed against the gossamer fabric.

Was she big enough to please him, she wondered with a critical frown and a tilt of her head as she turned sideways and studied her reflection in the beveled cheval mirror encased in ornately carved oak? A long, assessing look took in the matching lacy panties and thigh-high white hose that barely covered the rest of her. Was she pretty enough? Would the cobalt-blue of his piercing, thick-lashed eyes darken with desire when he saw her this way? Would his skin get all warm and tingly and his long, strong body go weak with yearning the way hers did at the mere thought of seeing him?

Or would he be disappointed?

Would she be less than he expected…or needed…or preferred?

Gaze fixed critically on her reflection, she saw a slim, slight woman with pale skin, average-size breasts and a long tumble of copper-colored hair that she'd had marginal success taming into a complicated tangle of curls on top of her head.

"It's your crowning glory, princess," her momma used to say when they would sit together in the pale evening light and Ellie had groused about the thick, unruly mass of it.

From the time she'd been a little girl, she had loved it when her mother had brushed her hair. The long steady strokes soothing her, lulling her into believing in fairy tales and happily-ever-afters.

"Someday a handsome prince will come and make me his princess, just like Sleeping Beauty, right, Momma?"

"Right, princess," her momma would agree, but with such a sad and guarded smile that Ellie had known her momma had thought there would be more frogs in her future than princes.

"Well, he came, Momma," she whispered to the empty room as the familiar ache of loss edged in to undercut her joy. "My prince came. I wish you could be here. I wish you and Daddy could be with us to-day."

Three years her mother had been gone. Time had eased the grief but not the sense of emptiness that had been compounded when her father died a month ago in March—and for the first time in her life, Ellie had been alone.

Turning away from the mirror and the melancholy

that threatened to overtake her, she thought, instead, of the man who would come for her in less than an hour—and she knew she wouldn't be alone any longer.

She walked to the closet and the carefully preserved wedding gown that awaited her. It was a dress made for a princess. Antique lace and virginal white satin hung in luxurious folds from a padded hanger. On the floor beneath the dress, age-softened slippers of the same pristine, shining fabric lay waiting.

"How pretty you must have looked in this dress, Momma," she murmured, and taking great care slipped it from the hanger. "How Daddy must have loved you."

Just as Lee would grow to love her.

She knew that he would. In time. Once he got to know her better. Once he understood that she was a woman, not a child. Once she showed him what she had learned from her parents about love.

And once she proved to him that she could be more than an obligation—which, she understood, was all she was to him right now.

Disappointed in that knowledge, but not defeated, she eased the dress over her head. She could make him love her. Even if she wasn't perfect.

Her gaze flashed quickly away from the mirror as she reached behind her back to fasten the many satin-covered buttons on the gown. No, she wasn't perfect, but she wasn't going to think about that. She wasn't going to let it interfere with her wedding day.

A twinge of guilt, the same one that had been niggling since Lee had explained why he was marrying her, suggested that she *should* think about it. Lee really didn't understand what he was getting into. She should have talked to him about it. But, since it was something that had never been talked about in this house, she didn't even know how to start.

In her entire life, she couldn't remember her parents ever saying the word. Doc Lundstrum had been the one to fill in the blanks for her. He'd been the one to put a name to the force that caused her to lose herself, to lose time, to lose memories and, it seemed, lose the right to live a normal life.

Epilepsy.

She closed her eyes. Swallowed.

No. It wasn't a word that had ever been spoken in this house. And it wasn't something that was easy to talk about with your prospective husband.

Yet, shouldn't he be armed with enough information to decide if he really wanted to go through with this?

He knows.

"He knows," she said aloud this time, working to convince herself as she reached for the fingertip veil crowned in baby's breath and white satin ribbon and allowed fear to trample over the guilt. Fear, prompted by an uncharacteristic selfishness and a buoyant hope, outdistanced the guilt and abetted her conviction.

"But *what* does he know?" she asked point-blank to the woman in the mirror. "What does he really know?"

Only what her momma had let him or anyone else know.

"Don't worry princess. No one saw anything."

"Saw what, Momma? What happened? What did I do?"

The answers had always been the same.

"It was just a little dream, baby. That's all that

happened. You just had a little dream and now you need to rest.''

She had no memories of life without the threat of seizures, just like she had no memory of what happened to her during one. She remembered only the aftermath, countless incidents of waking up in her bed, or other places, and the humiliation of not knowing how she had gotten there coupled with the headaches that followed and kept her down, sometimes for hours, sometimes for days.

The rush of frustration—of being totally out of control, totally vulnerable to the disease, of a loss of time and self that sometimes gave her nightmares—was far too familiar. She fought it back and settled the veil on her head.

And then she justified. Maybe it was best for now that Lee didn't know what to expect. She'd been four years old when he'd left Shiloh and Sundown, Montana, for college in Texas. As the years passed and he'd made those rare but treasured visits home, he'd never actually witnessed a seizure—at least she wasn't aware that he had. If he found out the whole of it before he got to know her for who she was…well. He'd get that look in his eye. The one she'd seen so many times before from others. The one that spoke of wariness and pity, or worse, ridicule and rejection. She would lose him before she ever had the chance to love him.

From downstairs, the grandfather clock in the hall chimed the quarter hour. Her stomach did a little flip-flop as she sat down at her dressing table and reached for a new tube of lipstick.

Less than an hour.

A lifetime of waiting and he'd be here in less than an hour.

That's all she had to think about today. Not the epilepsy, not the fact that her momma couldn't be with her, not the fact that her daddy couldn't give her away.

She brought the creamy, rose-colored gloss to her lips, surprised to see how violently her hand was shaking.

It's just nerves, she told herself, and frowned as the chimes sounded again.

She didn't think about reaching for a tissue so she was puzzled as, with a disconnected sort of awareness, she watched the unsteady motion of her hand lift one from the box and touch it to the light sheen of perspiration that had broken out across her brow.

And then she flinched when the chimes sounded again. Louder this time. Then again. Louder still.

Nausea rolled through her stomach in a heavy, arching wave.

"Why don't they stop?" she whispered, courting a shifting confusion she couldn't identify, fighting a creeping, disassembled anxiety that seemed to seep into her body from the outside in.

She tried to laugh at her bridal jitters but ended up closing her eyes to steady herself instead. When she opened them and met them in the tri-fold mirror, fear mushroomed and grew. She tried desperately to deny what she saw. A slight dilation of her pupils. A glassy mist covering eyes that looked vacant and unfocused.

She slowly looked away, and on a level she couldn't quite comprehend, watched the pretty silver tube of lipstick slip and, in slow motion, tumble end over end from her suddenly rigid fingers. It fell to her dressing table with a sharp, deafening clatter, then rolled to the sound of thunder before dropping with a booming crash to the floor.

The noise was piercing. The serrated, insistent clamor of the chimes got louder and louder until she clapped her hands to her ears and whimpered at the stab of pain the sound shot through her head.

"Oh, please," she pleaded, as the part of her brain that clung precariously to cognizant thought sounded the alert and she suddenly understood what was happening.

Seizure.

"No...oh, please, no. Not now. Not today."

But even as she prayed to a god that for whatever reason chose not to answer, a too-familiar metallic taste flowed into her mouth and she knew she was powerless against it. As she had always been powerless against it.

On shaking legs she rose to her feet just as the walls began a surreal dance that made them shrink, then swell, then close around her like a vise. She stumbled across the room, groping for the tall corner post on her four-poster bed, then gripped it with a soft cry as the noise exploded like crystal shattering against steel.

She clung to the bedpost, but her strength, like her hope, deserted her. On a level that was once distant and oh, so near, she felt the smooth, spindled wood slip through her hands like water, slide like cool rain against her cheek as she sank to the floor in a pool of white satin and crumpled lace.

A tear trailed down her temple and trickled into her hair as she lay back, stared at the ceiling and gave in to the void…defeated, defenseless, completely vulnerable in the darkness that took her.

The beauty of the day and the joy of her anticipation—gone. Her sense of self and time and hope—lost, just like her awareness of the moments that passed, of the actions of her busy hands that flitted clumsily to her throat to button buttons that did not exist, then button them all over again.

The childlike whisper that echoed through the empty room was hers. She didn't hear it. No one heard it.

No one heard the haunting loneliness, the tortured helplessness of the words she chanted over and over and over. "I'm sorry. I'm sorry. I'm sorry…."

Two

Four major rivers and at least a dozen minor tributaries snaked across the cracked plaster ceiling in room number six of Sundown, Montana's ancient and only hotel. Lee knew, because he'd been awake half the night staring at them. Staring and thinking and wishing there was a better way.

At 9:15 the next morning he still hadn't come up with one. So he'd dressed in his black suit and tie, stowed his luggage and the few belongings he'd brought with him from Houston in the back of his truck and he'd headed for Shiloh. And his bride.

A half an hour later, as he made the final turn up the narrow, rutted lane to Shiloh, a stray, two-week-old memory entered and softly settled.

I've ordered sunshine.

Despite everything that was wrong about what he was doing, one corner of his mouth edged up in a tight smile. It looked like Ellie was going to get her order filled on her wedding day.

Golden sunlight flickered through the budding aspen and shimmering evergreens flanking the high meadows, spreading warmth and the promise of summer over the slowly greening range, and gilding the vista of snow-capped peaks in the distance.

Easing back on the gas, Lee thought about the first time he'd made this trip up the mountain. He'd been ten years old. Ten going on fifty. He'd been angry, distrustful and so needy and full of fear that his gut still tightened at the memory.

Will and Clare Shiloh had changed all that. They'd saved him from the mean back streets of Denver. They'd brought him to Sundown. More specifically, they'd brought him to Shiloh Ranch. Twenty-three years later it had been Will who had brought him home again.

For what seemed like the hundredth time, he went over the string of events that had brought him back to the mountain. It always replayed the same—just like his conversation with his boss, Curt Tompkins.

"Is it more money you need, Lee? Hell, we can work something out. I don't want to lose you. And I can't believe you really want to leave Houston for some little inkspot of a town in Podunk, Montana."

Lee had hated letting Curt down. He'd been the manager of Curt's corporate spread for eight of the past ten years.

"Dave knows the ropes," Lee had said. "He'd be the one I'd look toward to take over. He can step in without missing a beat."

Curt had just shaken his head. "I don't get it."

And he never would, Lee had realized, so he'd simply stated the bottom line. "I owe Will Shiloh my life. Now I'm going to pay my debt."

He tipped his sunglasses up to the top of his head and squinted against the glare of sun bouncing off the truck's black hood. Yeah. He would pay his debt. Trouble was, Ellie was going to pay, too. It didn't help his conscience any to know that she was too young and too naive to realize what this little arrangement was going to cost her.

He knew though. Just like he knew that no amount of justifying could pit duty against guilt and balance the scales—or minimize his disappointment that Shiloh had come with strings attached.

He looked around him at everything that would officially become his in a little less than an hour. At one time owning Shiloh would have been an unreachable dream. He let go of a grim snort. "And look at me now."

He was a long way from where he'd come from. He'd like to think he was more than the boy who had cut his teeth on the bad side of the tracks. He hadn't understood it then. He hadn't cared that he'd been shuffled through an understaffed and inadequate social system by the time the Shilohs had found him. What he'd understood was hostility. What he'd understood was abuse. That had been life.

As young as he'd been, he'd known way too much about hunger. Way too much about pain. Most of all, he'd known about loss. He'd known it like a stray dog knew the hollow ache of an empty belly. And he'd known it every day of his life until Will and Clare had taken him in. Because they were kind people. And because, in their late forties, they had given up on having children of their own.

He let the truck roll to a stop at the top of the rise, eased it into park and thought about everything they had offered him—mountain wilderness, patience, hard work and endless understanding. In return he'd given them ten kinds of grief that first year. No matter what he'd done they hadn't sent him away.

"Run all you want, boy," Will had told him one midnight when he'd tracked him down near Butte. "Do your worst. You will always have a home here."

Significant. For the first time in his life he considered that he might actually be significant until, finally, he'd begun to believe that to Will and Clare, at least, he was.

Propping an elbow on the open window frame, he worried an index finger over his upper lip and stared at the house just the other side of the rise. The house where he'd known love. The house where the woman—barely a woman—waited to become his bride.

Ellie. Ellie, who he remembered as a sweet, laughing toddler. Then a shy little girl with a big bad crush on him with her guileless eyes and endless smiles. Ellie who was never supposed to be.

He remembered every moment of the day Clare had nearly died giving birth to the child she and Will had given up on the idea of ever having. He'd been fourteen—and he'd wanted to hate the wrinkled, mewling little thing that had almost killed Clare and had shaken the only firm turf he'd ever stood on. But from the first moment of her pretty pink little life, Ellie Shiloh had enchanted anyone who set eyes on her— Lee had been no exception.

Will and Clare had been amazed by her. They had sheltered this special gift that had brought a dawn sunshine into their twilight lives, moved heaven and earth to ensure that nothing would ever happen to the miracle that life had previously denied them.

It had been subtle and no way intentional, but Lee had felt the shift just the same. He was on the outside of the candy store looking in again. It had been a wake-up call. A reminder that as much stock as he placed in the Shilohs' love, he could only count on himself for the long haul. He'd also understood the deeper significance—Ellie had been born a Shiloh, and for as much as Will and Clare had given him, they had never offered him their name.

And it was only at times like these, he thought grimly—when he thought too much, brooded too much—that he let that lone fact bother him.

He drew in a deep breath of the fresh, mountain morning, adjusted his necktie, smoothed a hand down the lapels of his suit coat. And sat there, a million memories both drawing him to and keeping him from driving that final stretch into the valley.

Ellie had just had her fourth birthday when he'd gone off to college on a rodeo scholarship. She'd been eight, when at twenty-two, he'd received his degree in business management, sixteen when he'd come back to Sundown to mourn the death of the only mother he'd ever known.

And now Will was gone, too. Grief pressed down, cold and heavy. He flexed his fingers around the leather-wrapped steering wheel. It was just a month ago that Will had called him home. Just three weeks since he'd lay dying and extracted a promise Lee would give his own life to keep.

"You know she's special, our Ellie," Will had whispered as he lay in his hospital bed, shrunken and frail, the droning beep of the monitors seeming to ration out each heartbeat. "She's not strong like most folks, Lee. She's…delicate. She needs you, boy. And I need you to make sure nothing and no one ever hurts her or takes what we worked all our lives to preserve for her."

Delicate. That had been the word Clare and Will had always used in regard to Ellie's condition. On a gut-deep level, Lee had known that *delicate* didn't even begin to cover it. Admittedly, he didn't know what he should about her epilepsy. He'd never wanted to know. He wasn't very proud of that fact, but Clare and Will had never volunteered information, and frankly, that had been just fine with him. Hell. When the seizures had started, he'd been a kid himself. It was the best excuse he could come up with.

Honest truth? It scared him, what happened to her. It scared him for her. It scared him because he'd felt helpless…and excluded.

"Fever," Clare would say when a seizure would grab her, then she'd shoo him quickly out of the room. "Just a fever. Little ones have 'em all the time. She'll grow out of it."

Only she hadn't grown out of it. And he hadn't been around to see what happened to her. Once he'd made the break from Shiloh, he hadn't come home often and he'd kept the visits brief. It became easy— convenient—not to wonder or worry or feel guilty because it was happening to her and not him and that he still couldn't do anything to help.

Well. Now he was back. And now…now he would take care of her. He'd promised Will.

He hadn't thought once about saying no to Will's dying request to take over Shiloh Ranch. And, yeah, he'd figured that Ellie would come with the package—just not quite the way Will had in mind.

He'd been stunned when Will had asked the unthinkable.

"You're the only one I trust with her, son. You're the only one I can count on to do right by her."

Lee would have bled and died for Will Shiloh. For the giving man who had loved him without qualification, who had made him the man he was today. The man who was about to marry Will's pride and joy—because Will had asked him to.

He shifted in the seat, watched a curtain in a second-story window part, then fall back into place. It was going to happen. As sure as the sun came up it was going to set tonight with Ellie as his wife. He'd left the life he'd built in Texas, the friends, the women who had been a part of it.

"And you've sat here too damn long telling yourself you're doing Ellie wrong, when the fact is we're both getting everything we want," he muttered aloud, as if hearing it would make it all right.

Ellie wanted him—at least she thought she did. He wanted Shiloh, the place that had been in his blood, in his head, in his heart since the first day he'd set foot on the mountain. And Will had been right about one thing. Ellie did need someone to take care of her. It had just as well be him.

He slid his sunglasses back in place, eased the truck into gear and rolled down the last stretch home.

Home.

Where his child bride waited with trusting eyes and a hopelessly romantic soul.

Ellie was slow to answer his knock. When she finally opened the door, Lee was stunned all over again by the fragility of her beauty.

For a long moment he didn't speak—wasn't sure that he could. He just stood there, luggage in hand, flooded with foolish notions of fairy-tale princesses in shimmering satin and huge, enchanting eyes. And he wondered what the hell he was getting himself and her into.

She looked as if she'd just been kissed awake and the blush hadn't yet found its way to her pale cheeks. Beneath a delicate wreath of tiny white flowers and a shoulder-length veil, her red gold curls tumbled in an untidy fall from the top of her head, whispered in feathery ringlets along the porcelain column of her throat.

Those brilliant violet eyes were a misty shade of lavender and, he realized in a startling moment of alarm, as pale as the ashen pallor of her face—a pallor that he recognized came from pain.

"Ellie?" He set down his luggage and quickly went to her. "Are you okay?"

Her nod was slow in coming, her smile forced and breakable. Both lacked her usual exuberance. "I-I'll just get my wrap."

Her movements were calculated and careful as she reached for a shimmering white shawl of intricate lace and trailing fringe that was touchingly old-fashioned. Without asking, he took it from her unsteady hands, placed it carefully around her—too aware of the contrast of his big, work-roughened hands cupping her delicate shoulders. Acutely aware of her trembling.

He closed his eyes, let out a deep breath and accepted what was happening here. She wasn't well.

"Ellie," he said gently. "If you're not up to this—"

"I'm...fine," she insisted but without much strength in her words. "Really," she repeated, reacting to the frown of concern he knew was darkening his face.

She wasn't fine. That much was obvious. But this was new ground for him—as was the possibility that something other than illness could be responsible for that feverish look in her eyes. Maybe the reality of what was about to happen was finally hitting her. Maybe his virgin bride was simply scared to death.

And why the hell wouldn't she be? He hadn't exactly played the part of the love-struck bridegroom. Because he wasn't. And never would be. It didn't mean that he couldn't be kind, and it didn't mean that he didn't care about her. It was past time he gave her at least that much.

He smoothed a hand down her veil. "You know, we don't have to do this today. If you need more time to get used to the idea—"

"I don't...need time," she whispered, her speech uncharacteristically slow, her head down, her small hands clutched tightly together as if she had to concentrate to get the words out. "I've waited for you...all my life. I don't want to wait any longer."

The guilelessness of her admission both humbled and angered him. She deserved better than this. She deserved a white knight to sweep her away to a gilded castle in an enchanted forest. Instead, she was getting him. Her head was filled with illusions about who and what he was.

Well, he knew exactly what he was...and what he wasn't. He'd never been and would never be Lancelot material. And he would never be the man she needed him to be.

Still, this was going to happen, even though she was a total innocent—something he didn't think he'd ever been. It didn't mean, however, that he didn't have enough compassion to know she needed time.

"Ellie, there's no shame in admitting that you're...uneasy about this." He ran his hands in a gentle caress down her arms to cup her elbows.

She raised her head, her eyes beseeching. "No. Not uneasy. Excited." She smiled again, tragic and trembling. "I'm just excited."

When he shook his head, damned if she didn't try to put him at ease. "It will be all right, Lee. I'll make you happy. I promise I'll make you happy."

For a long moment he simply searched those glittering eyes that gazed up at him with such faith. He knew then that even though he couldn't give her what she wanted, he could at least give her something she needed. Whatever it took, he would earn her trust and her father's. Starting right now.

He touched his fingers to her cheek, smiled. "Let's go do this, princess. We can't let your sunshine go to waste now, can we?"

Tears glistened, at once hopeful and weary and achingly vulnerable. "No. We can't let it go to waste."

She smiled then, and a foreign and flooding warmth filled his chest. "You look beautiful, Ellie."

"So do you," she exclaimed breathlessly.

Against all odds he laughed and, prompted by instincts that mandated chivalry and grand gestures, tucked her small hand in the crook of his elbow.

"Well, now that we've got that established, your chariot awaits, m'lady."

Then he walked her to his truck and tried to ignore the unsteadiness of her gait and the unsettling notion that a thief other than anxiety had stolen the sparkle from her eyes.

For Ellie the wedding ceremony drifted by on a murky mist of excruciating pain. It was always like that after a seizure. The aftermath was a headache and a bone-deep exhaustion that often sent her to her bed for one or two days. She hated the helplessness, hated that it dictated how she could live her life.

Not today. She was not going to let it beat her today. She stood at Lee's side by sheer force of will, fighting to absorb it all, to stay on her feet, to feel the beat of her heart that assured her this was real. That she was here. She was with Lee, bathed in the blinding cylinders of sunlight refracting through the stained-glass window behind the altar. Smelling the sweet scent of the flowers he had thoughtfully placed in her hands. Watching the teary smiles of Martha Good, the pastor's wife, who stood as witness. Saying the vows she had waited her lifetime to repeat.

"By the power vested in me—" Pastor Good's lyrical voice reached through the fog and captured her full attention "—I pronounce you man and wife."

With every thread of strength in her, she fought to hold on to the day that would mark the beginning of the life she had always wanted.

"You may now kiss the bride."

She swallowed thickly, focused on Pastor Good's warm, encouraging eyes, then turned toward Lee. A gentle smile played on his beautiful mouth as he folded her in a loose embrace.

She tipped her face to his, wanting to draw it all inside—the moment, the magic, the feel of the plain gold band warming on the ring finger of her left hand and binding them together as man and wife. The burning heat in his eyes as he searched her face and drew her slowly toward him.

She fought the pain, battled to keep and cherish this moment forever. Their first kiss as husband and wife. *Their first kiss.*

She lost herself in the searching blue of his eyes, the promise of his breath, warm and mint scented against her cheek. They were so kind, those eyes, but it wasn't only kindness that she wanted from this man. She wanted always and forever. She wanted the magic that bubbled just below the surface every time she saw him. The thrill that raced along her nerve endings when he smiled. When he touched her. As he was touching her now.

As the pain touched her now.

She struggled to outdistance it. Willed away the crush of fatigue and thought only of him, of his lips brushing across hers, soft as a dream yet firm, commanding yet gentle. It was everything she'd imagined, many things she hadn't. She melted into the warmth of his mouth, loving the scent of him, the heat of him, the power inherent in his big body, the tender caress of his hands.

But, despite the magic, despite the defiance with which she clung to the moment, she finally accepted that this was a battle she could not win, a victory she could never lay claim to.

For the second time that day her body betrayed her.

That above all else she would remember about her wedding day as her world went black and she collapsed in her husband's arms.

"Ellie. Ellie-girl, it's time for you to join us again, honey."

She came around slowly. Struggled until she placed a face to the kind older voice. "Doc?"

"That's right, kiddo. Now open those pretty eyes for me so this wild man standing over my shoulder will know you're all right. There you go. That's the girl."

Even though the only light in the examining room spilled softly from the hallway of Dr. Lundstrum's office, pain exploded in her head when she opened her eyes. Pain, and a dawning realization of where she was, and where she wasn't. She wasn't at the church. She wasn't alone with her husband sharing the romantic picnic she had planned.

The physical discomfort suddenly paled in comparison to the pain in her heart. She flung an arm over her face to block the light and hide from the humiliation.

Doc's voice floated over the top of it all. "I want to give you something to take the edge off, Ellie."

"No," she whispered, defiance threaded with defeat. "No. It will make me sleep. I don't want to sleep. Not today."

A soft, affectionate chuckle followed a reassuring pat on her arm. "Now's not the time to be stubborn, little one. If we cut it today, you'll be up and around tomorrow. Otherwise, you know it could be another day or two before you're feeling better. *You* might be

able to take it, but frankly, I don't think your bridegroom can.''

Bridegroom. A hot tear welled up then spilled from
the corner of her eye, trailed down her temple and
got lost in the thickness of her hair. She hadn't wanted
Lee to see her like this. Not today. Not ever.

"Ellie, please." Lee's voice was gruff with worry,
softly pleading. "Let Doc give you something."

She squeezed back another tear, shamed and helpless to deny him. "Okay."

Doc touched her arm lightly. "Good girl. I want to
examine you first, Ellie, just to make sure I know
what we're dealing with here, then we'll take the
hammer out of that headache."

"She just fainted, right, Doc?" Lee demanded in
a hoarse and urgent whisper.

In the silence that followed, Ellie sensed Dr. Lundstrum's speculative frown. She opened her eyes, saw
the questions in the pale-gray eyes behind smudged
bifocal lenses, and the furrows above his bushy white
brows. She gave a small, pleading shake of her head.

Doc cleared his throat, let out a deep breath. He
patted his blunt-fingered hand on the round belly that
his sweet tooth had netted him over the years of en-
joying his wife's blue ribbon pies and smiled kindly
at Lee. "Why don't you wait outside for a minute?
Let me look your lady over. Then the two of you can
go home."

Ellie watched Lee's eyes darken as he scowled
from Doc to her. With grim reluctance he finally nodded, then left the room when Doc deliberately walked
him to the door. She heard his footsteps echo down
the hall as Doc turned back to her.

"I'm going to have to turn on the light now. I'm sorry."

She closed her eyes to the blinding glare as he flipped the switch, then shut the door behind him.

The minute they were alone she asked the question that had haunted her since she'd come to on the examining table. "Did I...did I—"

"You fainted, kiddo," Doc assured her as he lifted her limp wrist to check her pulse. His smile was gentle and indulgent. "You just fainted. Just like a blushing bride—or like someone who might be recovering from a seizure?" he suggested, then waited patiently while her silence confirmed his suspicion.

"Was it a bad one, Ellie?"

She started to shake her head. The pain slammed back full force. "No. No worse than usual."

"Long?" he prompted as he wet a cloth with cold water, laid it gently over her eyes, then reached for a blood pressure cuff.

"Two...three minutes, close as I can figure. I...I was getting ready for my wedding. I...I thought I could recover. I thought I could put it behind me...get through the ceremony and...and no one would... know."

Doc didn't say a word. He just rhythmically pumped the bulb, then watched the gauge with a practiced eye. He didn't have to say anything. He was thinking the same thing that she was. Physically it was the recovery time after a seizure that was the hardest to handle—at least it was for Ellie. The overwhelming fatigue, the unsettling sense of disorientation, the blinding headache took a toll. It had been beyond foolish to hope she could hide the residual effects from anyone. Foolish, but it hadn't stopped her from wanting to be whole for her wedding day.

With an unrevealing look, Doc removed the cuff, folded it into its sleeve on the wall and reached for a thermometer.

He squinted behind his glasses, then inserted the thermometer gently in her ear. "Have you been feeling okay otherwise?"

"Yes," she murmured, then restated, "Yes," when he leveled her a pointed look.

"Taking your meds on schedule?"

She frowned, gave a small nod, then flinched when the thermometer beeped and he checked her temp. "I hate them."

"I know." With one hand on her shoulder and one on her back, he helped her to sit up. He warmed the stethoscope in his palm, waited for her to steady herself then listened to her chest sounds.

She remained quiet throughout the rest of examination, holding the cold cloth to her eyes, knowing what was coming, ashamed of the answers she must give him.

He helped her lay back down then turned to prepare the hypodermic needle.

"This is going to bite a bit now," he soothed, swabbing alcohol on her arm. "Probably not as much as the bite your young man wanted to take out of my hide when I shooed him out of here."

She swallowed, waited.

"Lee's been gone from Sundown and Shiloh Ranch, oh, for quite a spell now, hasn't he?"

She held a breath, let it out and anticipated the questions she knew would follow.

"He does know about your epilepsy, doesn't he, Ellie?"

Another silence. "Sort of."

"Ellie—"

"I know," she preempted his gently scolding tone. "I know I should have talked to him. I know I should have let him know exactly what he was getting into. I...I just didn't want it to be today. I wanted today. I...needed today."

Doc set the syringe aside then covered the small puncture with a cotton ball and a strip of surgical tape. "He should know the details so he'll know what to expect." Folding her hand in his, he squeezed gently. "So he'll know how to react."

She couldn't stop the tears then. "Why does this...have to be a part of me?" Years of hurt and anger and a self-pity that she rarely gave in to spilled out in a broken demand. "And why...why couldn't I have had this one day without...without—"

"Sweetheart," Doc smiled, his voice wise and commanding yet soft with affection. "It's just one day. It's just one bad day in a string of good days that you know how to take one at a time."

"And I'll be stronger for it," she whispered with uncharacteristic bitterness.

"You are already strong. Stronger than anyone I know. And you'll get past this. Just like you always get past it. You and your young man will have a wonderful life together."

A wonderful life.

The words echoed, then drifted haphazardly around in her head until they tangled with everything that could get in the way of it becoming a reality.

Her reality was epilepsy. That alone was more than

enough to get in the way of Doc's prediction of a wonderful life. While her parents had done everything in their power to make it so, life, for Ellie, had never been wonderful. Life had been never knowing when or why a seizure would strike. Life had been home schooling to protect her from bold stares and whispering tongues, the cruelty of children who teased because they were afraid and didn't understand. While it would have hurt her parents greatly if they had known, life had also been isolating—both emotionally and socially.

It had been knowing that medication could lessen but not eliminate the seizures that stole her control and left her vulnerable and dependent and eroded little pieces of her spirit and her pride.

And life, quite often, had not been hers to live.

Like now.

She had a vague awareness of the drug taking a slow, slippery grasp on the pain, then a moment of simmering anger that her control had once again been stolen from her. Then even the anger drifted away with her consciousness—isolating her once again.

And then she slept—without a single dream of happily-ever-after.

"How is she?" Lee demanded when Doc Lundstrum finally strolled out to the waiting room where he'd spent endless time flipping through magazines he hadn't wanted to read, counting the worn gray tiles on the floor, then counting them all over again.

Old Doc just smiled. "She's fine. She's sleeping. It's what she needs right now. Take her home, let her rest and she'll be as good as new."

"Is it always like this for her?"

Doc laid a hand on his shoulder. "No, son. It's not always like this. You have to remember what she's been up against lately. Her daddy is gone barely a month. And now she's a wife. The excitement, the stress of being on her own, taking care of things...it took a toll. That's all. She'll be fine. You just let her rest now, and when she's up to it she'll tell you what she wants you to know."

The Doc had kind eyes, but he was too damn tight-lipped to suit Lee. "I want *you* to tell me."

Doc seemed to consider it, then shook his head. "It's not my place."

He couldn't help it. He blurted out the question that had been lurking like a black cloud since he'd caught her limp and lifeless body in his arms at the alter. "Is she...is this...hell." He scrubbed his hands roughly over his face. "What's it doing to her? Is it slowly killing her? Is she dying?"

"No," Doc assured him with a quick smile. "No. She's not dying."

A relief so swift it damn near drove the air from his lungs burst through him. While he was still recovering, Doc cast him an assessing look.

"This is something she's dealt with for a long time now, Lee. She's better prepared to handle it than you are. That will change with time, but for today, she's as humiliated as she is hurting. Both will pass, but she'll need you to get to that point. So, just tread carefully with her, son."

He ran a hand through his hair, still frustrated by all the unknowns, hating the thought of her in pain.

"Patience," Doc dictated with a slow nod. "It's what you both need right now. After you and Ellie have a talk, then you come back and see me and I'll fill you in on what you still have questions about, okay?''

No. It wasn't okay, but it was all Doc was going to give him.

Lee lifted Ellie, drowsy and mostly asleep, carefully out of the truck and headed down the walk to the house. She was like a little bird in his arms. Satiny soft, featherlight and so vulnerable it made his chest hurt. Her thready sigh fluttered like a butterfly's wings along the hollow of his throat as he shifted her slight weight more securely against him.

An April breeze rustled the satin of her flowing gown, stirred the downy curls at her nape while the late-afternoon sunshine she'd been so determined to shine on her wedding day, shot golden fire through her hair. The delicate little snore that snuffled out would have made him smile if he hadn't felt so frustrated and helpless and still so damn uninformed.

He looked down at the woman in his arms and accepted that it would be a while before she was up to talking—or for anything else for that matter.

Until today, the *anything else* had been a concern, yes, but still, a foregone conclusion. He was no monk. Even though he'd known she was an innocent, he'd also known he wouldn't be able to leave her that way. Look at her. What man could leave her alone? He'd planned on going slowly with her, but he'd had every intention of making her his wife in every way.

Now, though, now he wondered if maybe…well, now he wondered about a lot of things. Not the least of which was this intense and unfamiliar surge of feelings that went beyond obligation and duty. Hell, they even went beyond concern, and courted an unsettling notion that maybe there was more in jeopardy here than her health—like his lifelong contention that other than a physical relationship, he had little else in him to give a woman.

Large as life and with the clarity of crystal, a six-month-old conversation came to mind. The immediacy of it startled him. So did the content.

"You don't give a damn do you?" Sara O'Brien had fired the accusation at him like a bullet when he'd broken things off between them last fall. He'd been seeing Sara for several months. She was a nice woman and he'd enjoyed her company. But she'd developed feelings for him, strong feelings, and he'd known it wasn't fair to her that he couldn't return them.

Her brown eyes had been swimming with hurt and anger that he had apparently put there, and with what he'd strongly suspected was love—an emotion he had never trusted. He'd been up-front with her from the beginning. He hadn't been looking for forever. He'd thought she'd accepted the ground rules. By the time he'd figured out he'd been wrong, it was too late to do anything but back away—like he always backed away.

"You don't give a damn that I love you." She'd shaken her head, her soft, chestnut curls dancing around her face. "You never have."

"I'm sorry, Sara. I don't know what to say. I never meant to hurt you." And he *was* sorry, even if his words had sounded hollow.

She'd laughed, a harsh sound, tempered by grim acceptance and anger. "And that's the kicker, isn't it? You really don't want to hurt me. You stand there, and even now you cannot comprehend, cannot even fathom, why it hurts so much. Because you don't un-derstand love, do you, Lee? Don't understand it. Don't get it.''

She'd turned her back then and, squaring her shoul-ders, reached for her pride. ''You know what? I feel sorry for you. At least I know what it feels like to love someone. You never will. You'll never let your-self—and of the two of us, that makes you the most pathetic.''

Ellie stirred against him and dragged him away from that uncomfortable Texas memory to the woman in his arms. She tried to lift her head as he climbed the porch steps.

''Where—''

''Shush.'' He pressed his lips against her temple and concentrated on her. On what she was feeling, not on what Sara had known that he couldn't feel. Her skin was smooth and warm there, her hair as soft as silk and just as fine. ''We're home, Ellie. Just rest and I'll put you to bed.''

She looped her arms tighter around his neck as he reached for the door. ''This wasn't what I had in mind when…when I pictured you carrying me over the threshold,'' she murmured and snuggled closer.

A flood of affection filled his chest. His fairy-tale princess had been up for a fairy-tale wedding day. He wished it could have turned out that way for her. ''How about you just hold that picture and when you get to feeling better we'll do it right, okay?''

''Okay.'' Her misty response was so faint he barely heard her, yet with that one word, she gave her trust over to him completely.

Just like that. Just that sure. It rocked him, that

trust. More even than Will's entrusting him with the ranch had rocked him.

He hadn't come back to Shiloh planning to let Will down. And he wouldn't. Ellie—well, Ellie was a different matter. He didn't want to hurt her, but he pretty much figured it was a given. She had stars in her eyes. She saw him as romantic. She wanted a marriage built on love—not deathbed promises and payment of debts.

He wished, for her sake, that he could give it to her. Just like he wished he could have given something more to Sara. She'd been wrong, though. At least about one thing. He did understand love. He'd known love in this house. He'd just never learned how to give it back. He strongly suspected that it had never been a part of him in the first place—either that or it had been beaten or leached out of him long before the Shilohs had found him.

Whatever, it hadn't been a part of him then. It wasn't a part of him now. For that, for Sara and especially for Ellie, he was sorry.

Grim-faced, he climbed the stairs with her curled like a kitten in his arms. "But we'll get by, Ellie," he whispered into her hair. "We'll get by just fine."

He would take care of her. He would give her everything that he could…and knew in his gut that it would never be as much as she deserved.

Three

It was after midnight and Lee was in her virgin's bed.

He hadn't intended to be. He'd set his mind to making her comfortable, tucking her in, then doing some serious brooding.

He'd wanted to brood about all the things that he wasn't now and could never be for her. About this feeling of helplessness. Of knowing she was in pain. Of not knowing what lay ahead for her.

But more than he'd wanted to brood, he'd hated the thought of leaving her alone. So when he'd laid her down and untangled her arms from around his neck, her softly murmured ''Don't go'' had shot his intentions all to hell.

''Shush,'' he'd whispered to those big lavender eyes that were clouded with a medicated haze and a distant-but-very-real discomfort. She'd still managed to make him see how desperately she wanted him with her. "I won't go anywhere, Ellie. I'll be right here in the chair."

"In the bed," she'd insisted, and damned if that hadn't finally made him smile.

The lady knew what she wanted. And she knew how to get it. At least she knew how to get it from him.

He'd touched his hand to her face. "All right. In the bed, but let's get you comfortable first, okay?"

With grim determination, he'd gone to work on her gown.

His hands were big. The satin-wrapped buttons were small. And there must have been a hundred of them. He hadn't been prepared for that.

He really hadn't been prepared to deal with the sweet little body he'd uncovered underneath all that billowing white satin.

"I'm too small," she'd whispered as she'd lain there, too out of it to cover herself, yet very much aware that he was watching her.

It had taken several long, deep breaths to recover as he'd stood there by the bed, his hands full of yards of wedding dress, his chest full of a heart that was hammering like a sledge.

Sweet Lord. She was so tiny. So flawlessly exquisite against pale pink sheets in her white lacy underwear and sheer, shimmering stockings. He was stunned by the delicate, porcelain perfection of his bride and tried to think of how fragile she was, how breakable.

But all he could think of was that she was his. All the heat of that pale silken skin he'd uncovered belonged to him now. The romantic heart that had tucked a dainty blue hanky beneath the lacy edge of her thigh-high hose, his. The soft fullness of her breasts covered by sheer lingerie that had been sewn in the shape of flower petals. The shadow of downy, copper curls at the apex of her slim thighs.

His.

The picture came before he could squelch it. So vivid, so immediate it hit like a sucker punch. They were naked. It was full daylight. He wanted her in the sunlight. He wanted to see all of her. He was on his back in her bed, cushioned in down, covered by her; she was poised above him, that magnificent hair spilling down her back, her breasts rosy and wet from his mouth, her nipples pearled into tight little beads as she settled down on him, took him deep.

She moaned. It was soft but full of pain, and it snapped him back to the moment like a bucket of ice water. Board stiff, he studied her face, relieved that she appeared to finally be sleeping.

On a deep breath he laid her dress over a rocker in the corner of the room. Then he cleared his mind, settled his blood, slowed his breathing. With deliberate and calculated movements, he pulled the sheet and coverlet up to her chin, then sat down on the edge of the bed with his back to her. He loosened his tie, undid a couple of buttons. Elbows propped on his thighs, he dragged his hands wearily through his hair.

The reality of what he'd just done finally hit him. Like a bare-knuckled fist, it pounded dead center into the middle of his chest.

What had he gotten himself into? Worse. What had he gotten *her* into? A marriage that she'd really had no say in choosing, that's what. Sure, she thought this was what she wanted, but she was young. Naive. She was also absolutely dependent upon him.

And he wanted her.

He buried his face in his hands.

She was ill.

A slick ball of nausea rolled over in his gut.

"Lee."

He cleared his head and turned to her with a strained smile. "I'm right here, Ellie."

"Don't leave me."

Something inside of him tightened, then gave, like a bow when the tension was released—and just that fast, everything snapped into perspective. He couldn't exactly call it relief. What he could call it was acceptance.

He owed Will. That was the bottom line.

So he was struggling now because he'd finally figured out that he owed Ellie more than what he'd come to Shiloh prepared to give her. He'd thought it had been enough that he'd left his life, his work, his plans, that he'd made a sacrifice coming back to Shiloh— even as he'd told himself Shiloh was what he'd wanted, what he deserved.

Ellie...Ellie had just been part of the package. From a distance he'd been fine with that. He'd intended to be good to her. He'd intended to take care of her. He still did. He just hadn't realized until now what that might entail.

In sickness and in health.

From Texas the actual consequences of returning to Shiloh had been abstract. Workable.

Now...now it was getting damn sticky. He hadn't counted on the extent of her dependence on him. He also hadn't planned on—was having trouble coming to terms with—this knot of desire he'd been trying to deny since he'd come back two weeks ago and made arrangements for her father's funeral and her wedding all in the space of a week.

Her wedding.

His wedding.

In a way, he supposed, he'd viewed this marriage as a solution for him of sorts. Long ago he'd tired of the singles scene, the ritual dating dances, the plastic smiles and hungry eyes of the women who hadn't understood that the most he could give them was never as much as they had ultimately wanted. Women like Sara. Who he had hurt.

So, yeah, marriage had taken him out of that loop—efficiently, effectively. Good for him.

Not good for Ellie.

She needed more. And gradually, he was realizing that she deserved more.

"Lee?"

Resigned, he slipped out of his jacket, tossed it over her gown and eased down on top of the covers beside her.

"I'm right here." He folded her carefully into his arms.

"Promise. Promise you won't leave me."

If he hadn't been lying down, the whisper of desperation in her request, whether drug-induced or real, would have brought him to his knees.

"I won't leave you." He pressed a kiss to the top of her head, tucked her closer to his side. "I won't ever leave you."

And he wouldn't.

He was here. He was committed. He would stay.

She snuggled against him, all warm curves and unquestioning trust. An ache of emotion welled up behind his eyes, as acute as it was unexpected. It blindsided him, caught him completely off guard. He squeezed his eyes tightly shut then blinked back the sting of moisture that he refused to acknowledge was actually there.

He pressed his face into the cinnamon-sweet fragrance of her hair. Then he hung on. Just hung on to her as if she was suddenly his anchor—when he was supposed to be hers.

"I won't let you down," he murmured into the silk of her hair and tried to outgun these unfamiliar emotions she wrung out of him with absolutes. She was his obligation. She was dependent on him. And he'd promised Will.

"I promise, Ellie, I won't ever let you down."

Twilight came and went, and still he held her.

The grandfather clock in the downstairs foyer chimed the midnight hour, then one. He stared into the dark, his arms full of woman, his mind rejecting thoughts that just kept twisting back around into a stunning conclusion, no matter how hard he tried to divert them.

He'd come back to Shiloh to claim what was his. And yes, he'd come back to take care of Ellie. He hadn't come back because he needed her softness in his life. He didn't need anyone—never had. He didn't need this sense of home. He didn't need it…so bad he hurt with it. Refused to acknowledge that he was afraid to trust the good of it. The goodness of her and the weakness of needing everything she represented.

She murmured in her sleep, squirmed restlessly.

With his hand in her hair, he settled her. With his eyes wide open, he stared into the night and waited for morning to come—and with it, the detachment and distance from all these feelings that he counted on daylight to bring.

When Ellie finally awoke it was raining. It was also morning. She could tell even as she lay for a moment with her eyes closed, testing the weight of her headache and finding it mostly gone. The gentle patter of a morning shower rapped at her window, hurried by a wind gust, then abated again to soft little spattering taps.

She smelled the damp-earth scent of it and thought of her garden. She smelled the rich scent of musk on her pillow—and thought of her husband.

Eyes suddenly wide open, she stared first at the ceiling, then turned her head to find him. Gone.

The disappointment of it slowed the rapid beat of her heart. She touched her hand to the indentation in the pillow where his head had been. Cold.

But his scent lingered. And her memory stirred. He'd held her in the night. Warm strength. Gentle hands. Solid muscle.

A tear welled up before she could stop it. She'd wanted to give him so much more on their wedding night. She'd wanted to give; instead she'd ended up taking, like she always ended up taking from the people she cared about.

Rolling to her side, she pulled the covers up to her chin and glanced at the clock by her bed—10:15 a.m., Sunday, April fifteenth. Her first day as a wife. She was alone in her bed. And she was still a virgin.

Her heart sank as she watched the rain bead then run like tears down the windowpane.

That's how Lee found her.

He stood in the doorway, peripherally aware of the

garden of pink roses that adorned her bedroom walls, the fussy lace curtains, the four-poster bed covered with an acre of fluffy white down coverlet.

But it was the look of his bride that held him spellbound. Her back was to him, and she didn't know he was there. Her hair trailed behind her on the pillow like a tumble of shining ribbons as she lay watching the rain. The way she'd tucked her fisted hands under her chin was childlike and vulnerable—not so the soft curves that even all that down couldn't conceal. It was a woman's body that warmed the sheets. A woman's body that had snuggled against his through the night.

And it was a man that she needed this morning. A man who knew her limits and could impose a few of his own.

He had a handle on all that now. He had a handle on what she needed from him. She needed his strength and she needed his care. Beyond that, it was up to him to keep the lines from blurring and the mix from getting too intense until she was ready for more. *If* she was ever ready for more.

"Mornin', Ellie." His voice felt gravelly, sounded gruff as he stepped farther into the room and set the breakfast tray he'd prepared on the table beside her bed.

He watched her carefully as she lay there, her silence telling of how uncomfortable she was. With him in her bedroom? With the memory of him in her bed?

Or are you still sick, little one, and berating yourself because of it?

He settled a hip on the mattress at her side. "How are you feeling?"

She continued to stare out the window, avoiding his eyes. After a long moment she let out a breath that spoke as eloquently as her words. "I'm sorry I ruined our wedding day."

So, it was humiliation not nerves that kept her from facing him.

"Ellie...you didn't ruin anything," he insisted gently. "You were sick. It wasn't something you could help."

She slowly rolled to her back, then lay there, staring at the ceiling with eyes devoid of emotion. "It's never something I can help."

He'd witnessed her laughter; he'd witnessed her tears. Neither had as profound an effect on him as this blank look of utter defeat. He reached out, brushed a strand of hair from her cheek, a hundred questions rattling around in his head. For starters, what could he do, what could he say that would lessen the bruised look on her face? Bruised pride. Bruised spirit.

He didn't want to add more damage by hammering her with questions. He decided instead to let her set the pace, but he had to know one thing first. "How are you feeling...really?"

"Fine. Better," she amended when he slanted her a doubting look. "Really."

There was little he could do but take her at her word. "Are you hungry?"

She gave a little shrug that told him nothing and everything about her ambivalence. It also managed to expose one creamy white and very bare shoulder.

Sometime in the night she'd started fidgeting with her bra straps and he'd helped her out of it. The scrap of white lace, along with the pins that had held her hair in place, lay scattered on the floor by his feet. Both stirred his memory of a tantalizing glimpse of pale, perfect breasts, the alluring tips of berry-pink nipples bathed in moonlight.

He blocked the picture from his mind. "I think you should try to eat something." He cleared his throat and, dragging his gaze to her face, tried again. "There's enough food in the kitchen to feed threshers. Did you do all that? For me?"

She'd snaked an arm out from under the covers and, looking anywhere but at him, pinched the fabric of the comforter between her thumb and finger, pleating and repleating it. He covered her hand with his, stilling her nervous motions.

"Ellie, it's all right. I want you to stop feeling so self-conscious. When you're ready, we need to talk. But only when you're ready, okay?"

When she closed her eyes and swallowed hard, he turned her palm to his and linked their fingers together. "I'll take care of you."

She stared at their clasped hands. "I'm your wife. I'm supposed to take care of you."

He'd been taking care of himself for more years than she'd been alive, so the thought of a little slip like her looking out for him made him smile. He didn't think she'd want to hear that, though, so he suggested something he thought they could both live with. "How about we take care of each other?"

That finally earned him a small smile. He let out a breath that seemed to have been bottled up since he'd walked into the room and found her staring so forlornly at the rain. He squeezed her hand, then nodded toward the tray.

"Those wouldn't happen to be peach muffins?" he asked, even though he knew the answer.

Her smile blossomed and grew. He couldn't shake

the ridiculous notion that he felt as if the sun had come out.

"You baked them for me? Because they're my favorite?"

She nodded. "I remembered."

"There, see? You're already taking care of me. Nobody's made me peach muffins in..." He let the words trail off. The last time had been before Clare died. The thought turned the promise of a lighter mood back toward darkness. He could see in Ellie's eyes that her thoughts echoed his. "Well, let's just say that it's been a long time.... Now, how about you help me polish off a few?" he suggested, forcing a lightness back to his tone that brought her gaze to his. "I brought coffee, and I found some tea. Do you drink tea, Ellie?"

She smiled again, shyly this time. "We don't know much about each other, do we?"

Again he touched a hand to her hair. "We've got a lifetime to learn."

Everything in her expression told him that she liked the sound of that. Almost everything. The shadows in her eyes hid secrets that gave her pain and shut him out.

"Tea, please," she said, looking away. Clutching the comforter to her breasts, she concentrated on sitting up.

He quickly moved to help her. Gathering a trio of pillows, he propped them behind her back. She leaned into him, her weakness still obvious.

Her nakedness was also very evident as he reached around her and settled a pillow at the small of her back. The first touch was accidental, a brief brush of his fingers along the sleek line of her spine. The second touch was not. He shouldn't have done it. And yet, he couldn't stop himself. The temptation was too great. The indulgence too sweet.

His hand lingered there on the resilient warmth of her skin where the slight round of her hip met the indentation of her waist. It was like silk, that skin. It heated beneath his hand. Nothing short of her flinching could have stopped him from caressing that tender flesh, tracing the small ridges of her backbone as his hand slowly ascended.

She did not flinch. She sort of melted into him, her lips pressed to the hollow of his throat, her breath fluttering along his skin, heating his blood as her warmth filled his palm and her hair trailed like heavy lace along the backs of his fingers. He closed his eyes, savored it all, the scent of her, the supple resilience that was his virgin bride, before easing away.

Her eyes were huge and round, full of questions and wonder as they met and held his.

Are you going to kiss me?

Well. He really had no choice then. He cupped her jaw in his palm, tunneled his fingers into the hair at her nape and touched his lips to the petal softness of hers.

It was supposed to be a brush of a kiss, a hello, an invitation to trust. A promise that he would be here for her.

It turned into something more.

Her lips were warm, like her skin. Her response was instant. She opened for him, moist heat, incredibly soft and giving.

A spear of desire shot through him like fire.

He knew about practiced seduction, understood the art of guile. Neither was a part of Ellie's response. It was instinct, not practice that invited him inside. Honesty, not guile that sent lightning-swift pleasure singing through his blood.

No, she knew nothing of seduction. Yet he was being totally and thoroughly seduced. With an artless touch of her tongue, a breathless little shiver that filled his head with images and urges and hunger. The thought that she could take him to that edge so quickly only made him realize the care he had to take with her.

He was the one with the experience here.

He was the one with the control.

"I wonder..." he said, forcing himself to back away, to smile into her eyes and cater to her innocence and her needs instead of giving in to his own. "I wonder if your muffins taste as good as you do."

He'd never seen a woman blush before—at least not this prettily. It painted her cheeks a rosy-pink, then spread in a rush to color the flesh above the bedcovers, which her fisted fingers had let slip to reveal a tantalizing glimpse of high, round breasts, faintly marbled with a delicate network of translucent blue veins.

It took more than he'd thought he had in him to resist the urge to tumble her back on her pillows, slowly drag those covers to her waist and feast on the sight and then the taste of her. To take her sweet, pink nipple in his mouth, tongue it, graze it with his teeth and feel her body arch and yearn, ache and burn, slowly awaken to the woman she would become.

He gathered a necessary breath, a mandatory presence of mind.

He was way off the mark. This was not the time. This was not the direction he needed to go with her.

Not today. Maybe not for a very long time if he didn't get a handle on her illness and on her limitations.

And then there were his limits and the way she seemed to stretch them every time he was around her. He had to get a handle on that, too.

"Ellie, sweetheart, it would probably be a very fine idea if I got your robe."

Ellie blinked once, slowly, then wet her lips, trying to capture the taste of his mouth, searching to read the dark look in his eyes, longing to know him as a bride should know her husband on the morning after her wedding.

Questions. She had so many questions about what they would do together. In this bed. How he would touch her. Where he would kiss her. She had so many fantasies. Many of them were nurtured by the book she'd ordered by mail so she would know how to be a wife to him. Many more were fostered by just looking at him and knowing he could probably teach her more than she could ever learn from that book.

"In the closet," she said, instead of telling him what she wanted. Another kiss. The touch of his hand. On her bare skin. On her naked breast.

She didn't know how to tell him those things. At least, that's what she told herself. The way he'd reacted when he'd kissed her—oh, my. It seemed they'd been communicating just fine. The truth was that she was a coward. She was his wife now, but the part of her that kept her from being so many things still kept her from being his woman. Not just the physical part of her illness, but the part that affected how she felt about herself, how she felt about who she was and what she was. The part that made her different. The part that made her vulnerable to the whim of misfiring brain waves and shook her confidence.

She watched him rise and walk across the room. Watched the perfectly strong, long length of him, the breadth of his shoulders, the dark satin of his hair, the deep-blue of his eyes when he turned back with her robe, and felt a throbbing ache low and deep inside her.

In the wake of what she recognized as wanting rode a stark reminder of reality and regret. She quickly looked away. She should have told him everything. She should have prepared him. It hadn't been fair.

Even before she met his eyes again, she felt the loss a full disclosure would bring. His kiss had said he wanted her. But would he want everything that came with her?

Guilt settled like a stone.

I won't ever leave you.

That's what he'd said last night. Even through the medicated haze, she remembered. That's what she'd begged for. That's what he'd promised. She wouldn't hold him to it. She knew that now. Now that she realized she hadn't really wanted him at any price. She'd wanted him at the price of love. At the price of forever. But after yesterday and last night, she realized she did not want him at the price of her pride.

So she would tell him. Everything.

But not now.

Not naked.

She couldn't talk to him about it naked. She felt too vulnerable. And that vulnerability, like her faint but lingering headache, justified her decision to stall what was unavoidable for just a little while longer.

* * *

Ellie had been worried about her chores, so Lee had left her with orders to please stay in bed while he took care of things for her. He'd needed the distance. He'd needed the physical labor to clear his head. So he'd fed the chickens, gathered the eggs, then checked on the handful of horses stabled in the barn. The rest of the herd grazed free on the open range.

Going through the motions had been both grounding and disconcerting. It reminded him of years past, the satisfying simplicity of physical labor when it had been just him and Will and Clare. It reminded him of what his life no longer was—high tech and profit driven. Oddly, he felt equal measures of contentment and loss.

Mainstay, the corporate cattle operation he'd managed for Curt outside of Houston, had been his life for the past ten years. He'd run the bulk of the operation from behind a desk with the assistance of the Web that kept him apprised minute by minute of the markets—the high-tech software that defined to a pencil-sharp point rate of gain, profit and loss, market trends. It had been a high-pressure position that he'd competed to get, worked like a dog to keep. And while it would never erase a starving street kid's memories, it had given him what that kid had never had. Financial independence. Some shrewd investments and a knack for playing the markets had cemented his future.

"I thought you liked it here," Curt had protested in a last-ditch bid to convince him to stay.

"I don't just like it, I love it. I love the competitiveness of it. The orderliness, the cutting-edge technology. But I also hate it," he'd confessed, trying to help Curt understand. "I hate the loss of hands-on management. I miss the physical labor—it's cleansing and real…like the creak of saddle leather and the scent of horses."

He'd laughed when Curt had looked at him like he'd gone over the edge. "Okay, okay. I know it sounds sappy, but I miss the sense that I play a critical role in the day-to-day operations of a working ranch. Shiloh will give all that back to me."

And he could give to Shiloh what Will hadn't been able—or had never wanted—to give. He could make it into something other than a hang-on-by-the-skin-of-your-teeth proposition. He could ease Shiloh into the twenty-first century. In the process, he could preserve a way of life that was becoming as obscure as a working horse in an SUV age.

He looked around him at the outbuildings that hadn't seen a coat of paint in four decades, the hulking giant of a house that had been built at the turn of the twentieth century and had benefited from very few updates since. He had the capital to invest in repairs, improvements and innovations. He had the desire to keep the ranch intact. And he had the will to say no to the pressure to sell out to the moneymen who'd been sniffing around. If they had their way, they would own Shiloh, then turn it into their personal game preserve or subdivide and make millions selling little pockets of paradise and populating the mountains with Hollywood types gone country. Well, that wasn't going to happen. Not on his watch.

He stepped onto the back porch, made a note to get to work on both the front and back porch floors and tried to understand why Will had never accepted his offers to help out.

"Don't need your money, boy," he'd say in that soft, slow cadence that promoted trust and relayed pride. "We're doin' fine. Me and Mom and the girl. Sure would like to see your face, though. Know you're a busy man, but when do you think you can get home for a spell?"

He opened the kitchen door, set the bucket of eggs on the table and felt the guilt eat a little deeper. He hadn't come home often enough. He'd known it then. He knew it even more keenly now. Now that it was too late to do anything but miss them.

The house was comfortably quiet as he washed his hands, then dried them on a towel that had been looped through the handle on the refrigerator door. It was the same refrigerator that had been sitting on the same worn gray-and-white linoleum flooring twenty-three years ago when he'd come to Shiloh.

After pouring a mug of coffee, he leaned back against the counter and studied the room. It had never seemed shabby to him back then. Even though Ellie obviously worked to keep the house clean and welcoming, he couldn't get over how sadly neglected it seemed now. How neglected everything seemed.

When a floorboard creaked overhead, he realized that he'd been listening, hoping even, for some sign that Ellie was up so he'd have an excuse to go check on her. Harder to admit, despite his concentration on his chores and his plans, she hadn't been out of his mind for a moment since he'd left her in her bed. All pretty and pink and kissable.

With a disgusted breath he looked up, took another sip of coffee. Then he made an honest effort to tuck her neatly into a cubbyhole alongside the rest of duties on his list. Fix everything in sight—including both porch floors, paint the house, check the herd, take care of Ellie. Just take care of her. She was fragile, she was vulnerable, and that's what she needed from him most. His care.

He knew that. And yet, he hadn't—not for a minute—stopped thinking about her lying in her bed, her expression open with wonder, inviting him to kiss her again. Inviting him with her velvet eyes to do all the things he'd been wanting to do and more.

He didn't like it much. He didn't like it that he couldn't get her out of his head but he could—and would—handle it. Starting right now. He would do what Will had asked him to do. He'd take care of her.

Setting the mug aside, he walked slowly into the living room, determined to do just that. He hesitated for only a moment before gripping the worn oak banister and ascending the stairs.

"Ellie?" he called out softly as he rounded the corner in the upstairs hallway and walked into her room. The bed was empty.

He heard water running in the bathroom and followed the sound. It made sense that she would want to bathe. It would also make sense that if she weren't feeling up to it, she wouldn't tackle it on her own. Or would she? She would be shy about asking for his help. She would be modest. And if she'd known that he was picturing her sweet-scented and naked and wet, she'd have been running for her life.

Disgusted with himself and determined not to shock her, he walked slowly toward the bathroom door at the end of the hall—and found it mostly open. He was about to knock, about to ask if she was doing okay, when he saw a shadow of movement and she walked into his field of view.

Her back was to him. She was wrapped from neck to ankle in her pink robe when she stopped beside the deep, claw-foot tub that was slowly filling with hot water. With a grace and unconscious sensuality that made his pulse leap, she swept that riot of curling copper hair into a loose knot on top of her head and secured it with a gold clip. Then, still unaware that he was watching her, she undid the belt of her robe.

He should have left her to her privacy then. At the very least he should have let her know he was there. But he couldn't seem to move, was beyond speech as the soft chenille slid from her creamy white shoulders, slipped down her slender back, and caught low on her hips before pooling in a drift of pink at her feet.

Four

She was, in one very inadequate word, exquisite. Her skin was pale and flawless, her neck long and graceful. Her waist was small, like the rest of her—the flair of her hips woman soft, her legs sleek and supple. Twin dimples saucily winked at him from above her sweetly rounded bottom, drew his gaze, stirred his sex—as did a strawberry-shaped beauty mark riding a little left of center at the small of her back. He wanted to touch her there with his lips, stroke her there with his tongue.

Mine, he thought again, unaccustomed to the hard, swift punch of possession that swamped him.

He wasn't conceited and he wasn't blind. Women found him attractive. The women he'd taken as lovers had been sophisticated and beautiful—and they hadn't looked at him with forever in their eyes and a trust that ran river deep.

Just as none of them had never moved him as she did. None of them aroused him like she did. And none of them—not even for a moment—could make him forget who he was and who he wasn't and what he wasn't prepared to give.

He had to back away from her. Now. But then she leaned forward and turned enough in profile to show a teasing glimpse of one sweetly rounded breast. He was already semihard when the sight of that velvety pink nipple turned him to stone.

And he wasn't going anywhere.

There was nothing about her that wasn't a bewitching paradox of eroticism and innocence. And when she reached across the tub, tested the water with a slow swish of her hand, then poured a thick, creamy liquid from a clear glass bottle, he nearly groaned. Had to tell himself to breathe when she stepped over the rim and eased into the water.

She leaned back as the tub filled slowly, scenting the air with the fragrance of vanilla. Clouds of bubbles built until they reached her waist, flirted with the undersides of her pretty breasts.

As he watched, her nipples tightened.

He damn near went to her then, knelt beside her, touched her where the water didn't, and where it did.

It would embarrass her, he told himself. Just as his watching would embarrass her. He knew he should look away. He was her husband, yes, yet he felt like a voyeur, invading her privacy, breaching her trust. At least he thought he was until, with a languorous yet deliberate sigh, she turned her head and looked him straight in the eye.

His heart thumped like the recoil of a shotgun. Before he could recover, it rocked him again, slamming against his sternum, pumping blood to his head in a dizzying rush.

She blinked once, held his gaze for a long, searching moment, then slowly turned her head, draped her arms over the rim of the tub and let her eyes drift shut.

Shock held him there, right where he stood, for several long, mind-numbing seconds.

She'd known.

She'd known he was watching her.

A jolt of something closer to pleasure than surprise shot through his blood—until it occurred to him that he might have underestimated her.

Maybe he'd been a fool to think she'd come to him a virgin. She was very beautiful. And he seriously doubted that the young men of Sundown were blind or stupid. He remembered how he'd been at nineteen. He remembered what he'd wanted from a woman then.

He knew what he wanted right now.

He took a long, lingering look at all that creamy wet skin until looking was no longer enough.

Lust teamed in a dicey alliance with a hard, tight clutch of jealousy and took over, told him what he wanted to hear. The hell with being careful with her. The hell with what she needed from him. She'd invited this. She'd stripped for him, posed for him. Woman sure, seductive, inviting.

"You don't have a clue what you just invited, princess," he uttered under his breath.

Good intentions or no, he'd be damned if he'd feel guilty for reacting to her like a man. She wasn't Lolita, and he wasn't a lecherous old coot. He was thirty-three years old—and he wanted his wife.

He shoved the door all the way open, let it slam against the wall with a satisfying smack.

Her eyes were open now, growing wide and round as he crossed the room and loomed over her. He didn't even attempt to hide the hunger when he swept his gaze over the part of her that the bubbles covered and the part they didn't.

Mine was all he could think again, when he leaned over her and braced his hands on the tub's edge at either side of her head. Satisfaction coiled in his gut, as fierce and sharp as a whip, when she crossed her arms over her naked breasts and sank a little lower in the water.

She wasn't feeling so sure of herself now.

You play with fire, little girl, you're gonna to get burned.

Only he was the one burning. He was the one who could barely breathe, could only think of the silk of her, the heat of her, the need of her.

He followed her down as she sank deeper, caging her in. Biceps bunching, he lowered himself until his mouth hovered a breath away from hers.

"Open," he demanded, not checking the growl, not denying the need as he roughly captured her mouth. Once, a quick, primitive nip of lips and teeth. And again, to make it clear that she'd roused the beast in him—and that she'd better be prepared to deal with it.

Then he wasn't acting on his needs, but reacting to the force of them. And just like his reason, his resolve got lost somewhere in the pool of pink cloth that lay, along with her innocence, on the floor by the tub.

Desire rocked through his blood at the taste of her, shot to oblivion any concern. The silky heat of her mouth, the giving resilience and the shimmering threads of her startled breath, fed his need to an inferno.

Her strangled little gasp spoke of her inexperience as he found her tongue, stroked it then drew it into his mouth. The restlessness of her trembling sigh told of her awakening desire…and a burgeoning awareness of a woman's control over a man.

Control.

A flash of cool blue broke through the fiery-red haze clouding his eyes and his judgment. He didn't lose control. Not like this. Never like this. And he'd never given it over to a woman.

He pulled away far enough to break the contact of flesh on flesh. The warm, hurried pulse of her breath beat in short, quivering bursts against his lips.

He meant to leave her then but couldn't stop himself from looking his fill. She was drenched in color and fragrance. A dew of steamy bathwater and a dawning sensuality painted her skin, from her cheeks to her breasts, a rosy pink glow.

When her eyelids fluttered, he willed his hammering heart to settle. But she wasn't done with him yet. Her eyes opened with a slow, languid sensuality, and her tiny pink tongue slipped between kiss-swollen lips to lick and taste, savor and soothe.

Even as his heart slammed into race speed, an intense wave of tenderness swamped him and finally accomplished what that damn control he so valued hadn't been able to. It cleared his head.

He had to get out of here.

He had to do it now before he said the hell with taking care. He'd never wanted so badly. He'd never needed this much. Hell, he was still only a deep breath away from stripping off his clothes and crawling into that old claw-foot tub full of bubbles and Ellie.

Ellie. She'd made him forget who he was dealing with. She'd made him forget that he had to take care. She couldn't handle what he had in mind. He wasn't even sure that *he* could.

He made himself push away. Made himself stand, walk out of the room and away from the house and the knowledge that he'd almost taken her in that moment—without regard to her innocence or her health.

And he didn't hate himself nearly enough.

It was a long time before Ellie gathered the nerve to walk downstairs. Her headache was completely gone. The sluggish aftereffects of the pain medication had pretty much worn off. As much as she hated knuckling under, she was glad now that she'd let Doc talk her into the shot. She wasn't as sure how she felt about her behavior when she'd discovered Lee watching her prepare for her bath.

Or how she felt about that kiss.

One thing she was sure of. After she'd gotten past the fierce look on his face and the crushing surprise of his mouth on hers, she'd liked it. A lot.

Places inside her—well, she still got all warm and achy and weak just thinking about the places in her body his kiss had affected.

She felt her skin flush beneath her faded jeans and her soft white T-shirt as she gathered her hair at her nape with a wide gold clip and made her way to the kitchen that she knew was empty.

She knew it was empty because she'd heard the back door creak open, then shut right after Lee had left her a little more than an hour ago. Since then she'd caught glimpses of him outside. His face had been set in a hard, grim line as he'd gone to work on the woodpile by the garage.

Why he'd thought he needed to split wood in April when Don Ferguson, the next-door neighbor, had made sure she'd had enough to get her though any cool spring evenings was beyond her.

She couldn't say that she was sorry Lee had chosen to work himself into a glistening sweat, though. Especially after he'd taken off his shirt, then mopped his brow and his flat belly with it.

She'd watched him from her bedroom window. All that woman heat he'd set aflame when he'd kissed her in the tub had warmed up all over again. His shoulders were so broad. His chest was beautifully covered in an interesting pelt of soft brown curls. And lower, where his belt buckle met his abdomen just below his navel, his belly was taut and hard—like the corrugated roof on the machine shed. All firm and fine and…well. She hadn't been around many men in her life. Not young men, at any rate. Not any naked men.

Not that Lee was naked—although she sure had been wondering about him that way. And not that he was a young man. Not like John Tyler was young. Young and stupid and mean.

Frowning, she located her prescription bottles in the cupboard by the sink, uncapped them and tipped the appropriate doses into her palm. As she filled a glass with water and swallowed the medication, she tried not to let long-remembered hurts bother her. But they were always there. The memories. The taunting. The malicious smiles of a boy she'd wanted for a friend way back when. It had turned out that he'd only had one thought about her.

"What's the matter, Ellie?" John had asked, all sweetness and smiles when she'd finally gotten brave enough to stay put when he'd approached her one morning after church. "Cat got your tongue? Or did you bite it off throwin' one of your fits?"

Okay. So he'd only been twelve at the time. And he'd been a boy, not a man—so had his buddies who had stood by laughing like loons at her expense. It hadn't helped when his mother had made him apologize, then dragged him to the car by his ear. It hadn't helped when her own mother had held her to her breast when she'd cried.

"Ignorance, Ellie. The boy's only excuse is ignorance. Everybody's got something about themselves that they don't like. Sometimes the way they go about making themselves feel better is to make other people feel bad."

It hadn't been the first time someone had succeeded in making her feel bad about herself and mortified about how she was perceived by others. But it had been one of the few times she had made a real effort to be accepted by her peers, so it hurt all the more because she'd been foolish enough to open herself up to the attack.

She'd quit begging her mom and dad to let her go to regular school that day. And she'd quit making eye contact with anyone but the people she completely trusted.

Five years later, when John Tyler had asked her to go for a ride with him after church to get an ice cream cone and then to watch the fireworks at the Fourth of

July celebration, it had been easy to turn her back and walk away.

John and everyone like him had had all the shots at Ellie Shiloh they were going to get. She no longer cared what they said about her. Besides, she had always known who she trusted. And who she loved. She loved Lee. It had always been Lee, from her first memory of him holding her on his knee and she'd smelled horses and leather and sensed the strength that had made him a man, she had loved him.

And now she was his wife.

At least in name.

She walked to the fridge, opened the door and thought about that kiss again. Of how she'd started out feeling a little fearful, a lot exposed and ended up feeling...she wasn't sure what she'd been feeling. Wanting. Restless. Yearning for something she couldn't explain but knew would be wonderful. She hadn't wanted that kiss to end. She hadn't wanted him to leave her like that. All hot and wet and alone.

Cool refrigerated air washed against her heated checks as she thought of what she'd done to entice him.

She still couldn't believe how bold she'd been. She'd heard his footsteps on the stairs; she'd known he'd come looking for her. Her first thought had been to quickly shut the door. Her second—her second thought brought heat to her cheeks again.

Leave it open. Let him find you. Let him see you.

She'd suddenly realized that she had wanted him to come to her. And when he had, and he'd just stood there, thinking she hadn't heard him, some instinct had told her what to do. How to act to make him want her.

It had become important suddenly that he want her. It had been a necessary risk of her pride. And she'd been shameless. She'd been brazen and breathless as she'd slipped out of her robe. Knowing he was watching. Hoping he'd been wanting.

Except for Doc, no man had ever seen her naked. Even her mother hadn't seen her that way after she'd started developing. She'd felt too self-conscious.

She hadn't felt self-conscious today. She'd felt... like a woman. His kisses had told her he'd thought of her as one, too.

Until he'd walked away.

She looked at the wall clock, saw it was close to noon and gathered the cold fried chicken she'd made the day before yesterday.

He'd looked hard and angry and distant when he'd walked out of the room. That's the part that worried her most. What had he been thinking?

It didn't take much imagination to come up with some possibilities. Had he suddenly seen what everyone else saw when they looked at her? Had he thought, *What am I doing?* Worse, *What have I done? I married Ellie Shiloh. Epileptic Ellie Shiloh. What have I tied myself to for the rest of my life?*

Maybe Momma had been right, she thought, as an anger that lived deep in a forgiving soul had her hands trembling and her heart thumping at her breast like a raging fist. Like John Tyler, maybe Lee was just another frog disguised as a prince and she'd been a fool to expect he'd be any different.

Tears threatened to spill over into her fried chicken. Tears of outrage, injustice and a disappointment that sliced deep to the marrow.

"We need to talk."

She jumped at the sound of Lee's voice, startled that he'd climbed the back porch steps and was standing just the other side of the kitchen screen door. It was a measure of how lost in thought she'd been that she hadn't heard him.

But he was here. Big and beautiful, the hair at his nape and forehead spiked with sweat, the shirt he'd thrown on still hanging loose and unbuttoned. He looked hostile and dangerous. His blue eyes were as dark as a storm cloud and sent her already galloping heart into a flat-out run.

Her biggest surprise was realizing that it was anger, not fear that sent her heart racing. She had a little thunder to deal with too, thank you very much, and he was going to be on the receiving end.

"You're right, we do," she agreed, pleased with the startled look on his face and the fact that she'd put it there.

The phone rang before she had a chance to rattle him even more.

And Lee *was* rattled. He'd spent the better part of an hour trying to work off about a semi load of sexual frustration with an ax and an ugly attitude.

All he'd gotten was tired. And all he'd been able to think about was her.

Very wet.

Very willing.

She still didn't have a clue what she'd invited, or she'd be running like hell instead of standing there ready to face off with him in a game that she couldn't possibly win because she didn't know the rules.

And that, he'd decided as he'd whacked away, was the problem. He didn't know the rules anymore, either. She'd changed them. With her sweet little body, her vulnerability and her ability to make him feel…feel what, Savage?

He didn't know. He just knew he didn't like it. Was absolutely clueless about how to deal with her, what he felt for her, what he wanted from her.

In one day—twenty-four hours—she'd turned him inside out, flipped him upside down and spun him sideways.

He had to have some answers—about the epilepsy, about her expectations, her limitations, so he could get a handle on all this…this stuff that was rattling around in his head. Stuff he didn't understand. Stuff that made his chest hurt, made his head hurt. Stuff he'd never had to deal with before and didn't much like dealing with now.

Stuff that had made him lose it earlier. Yeah. He'd flat-out, combat-ready, lost it. His hands still shook when he thought about how he'd practically attacked her. Hell, he *had* attacked her, there was no *practically* about it. And outside, just now, he'd damn near lopped off a foot because he'd been thinking about her…about her mouth, about her breasts—

He was doing it again.

He drew a deep breath, unclenched his fists and made himself level. They would talk. He would get his answers—and then he would decide how this was going to play out.

"Shiloh Ranch," he heard her say as she snatched the receiver up on the second ring.

"Oh, hello, Pastor Good."

Lee watched her smile, then respond to whatever the good reverend was asking on the other end of the line.

He curbed his impatience and waited out the call.

"Oh, yes. Yes, I'm feeling much better today. Thank you."

She listened, smiled again, then blushed. "He's fine. Yes. He's right here. I was just putting out lunch.... Oh, no, of course you aren't interrupting.... Okay. Yes. And thanks for calling."

She hung up the phone, stared at it for a moment, then wiped her palms nervously on her jeans. "Pastor Good," she explained unnecessarily as she turned, making a vague gesture toward the black wall phone. "He wanted to know..."

She trailed off, and Lee felt compelled to prompt, "Let me guess. He wanted to know the same thing that Doc Lundstrum wanted to know when he called this morning while you were still sleeping. Then there was the call from old Mrs. Porter who had heard from Mrs. Stiller down at the library and Mrs. Waldrop over at the Christian Women's Club and, let's see, who else—Hap Callihan down at the hardware store. Lord, I thought he died a couple of years ago."

He was frowning and didn't know why. He should be grateful that people checked in on her. Instead he felt excluded. They knew things about her that he didn't. They knew how to take care of her better than he did. He didn't know a damn thing. But he was going to find out. Starting right now.

"Look, Ellie—"

Before he could finish, the phone rang again.

She started, her eyes big and round as she stared at him, waiting for him to continue as the phone rang a second time.

He stalked over, snagged the receiver off the hook and shoved it toward her. Then he dragged his hands through his hair, resigned to wait out another call.

"Um, Shiloh Ranch," she said after a long heartbeat. "Oh. Hi, Buzz. Good. I'm good. Thank you... No. No, I don't have a list. No. I've got everything...actually, um, Lee should be able to pick up anything I need from now on."

Lee frowned as he listened to her end of the conversation.

"Oh, Buzz, of course you can still come out and see me. Whenever you like. Yes. What would I do without our cribbage games? Right. Okay. I'll see you sometime soon."

She hung up, turned to him again with another embarrassed little lift of her shoulders. "That was Buzz."

"Stop & Shop Grocery Store Buzz?"

She nodded.

"He has to be pushing eighty...and he's delivering groceries to Shiloh?"

She turned abruptly, showing him the view he'd been trying not to appreciate the hell out of since he'd walked into the kitchen and found her nose in the refrigerator and her sweet little butt pointed his way.

"He started when Momma got sick and Daddy was busy with foaling," she said reaching into the refrigerator and digging out a bowl of potato salad to go with the chicken she'd already set on the table. "We needed groceries one day, I called and asked if anyone happened to be coming out this way and would he be willing to send out an order. Buzz ended up bringing it out, and he's been delivering groceries ever since when we needed them."

He was about to ask why it was necessary for decrepit old Buzz to deliver their groceries when she met his eyes, looked quickly away, then started fussing with the tea towel that hung over the handle on the old gas stove.

Because she couldn't drive, that's why, he realized a split second later. He understood then, on a level that made him stop and really consider the implications, another facet of her limitations. It was pretty much common knowledge that, by law, the probability of seizures prevented many epileptics from possessing a valid driver's license. And what till now had been a tidbit of information that had never affected him or his life affected him deeply.

How would it feel, he wondered with a knot of realism tightening in his chest, to lose a basic freedom that he'd always taken for granted? How would it feel to be denied the excitement of plopping down a fee and trying to pass a driving test when you were sixteen years old? How would it feel to know you were breaking the law if you drove without a license to just get to work or to school or to the grocery store?

He studied her face, saw in her eyes both the pride she was entitled to and the shame that she had no reason to claim.

"Okay," she said into the silence that settled, "you wanted to talk."

Then she blushed from the roots of her hair to the pale flesh that disappeared beneath the round neck of her T-shirt. She'd dropped the tea towel. In fact she stood utterly still. The rise and fall of her breasts beneath her shirt was the only indication she was breathing.

He'd so been worried about how he would handle the information about her epilepsy. Well, what about her? How would talking about it make her feel? It would be hard for her. Harder than he'd ever realized.

It would hurt her. Leave her feeling exposed and vulnerable and, as she so often was, dependent on someone else's decision on how they would deal with the information. Would he reject her? Pity her? Use it against her? Worse, would he ridicule her as he was sure so many had?

Hell. He didn't want to think about it anymore. And he didn't want to talk. He wanted to hold her. He wanted to kiss her. Long and deep. Then he wanted to carry her to bed and do things to her that would guarantee she'd forget, at least for the moment, everything that put that look in her eyes.

And accomplish…what, Savage? *He'd* feel a hell of a lot better, yeah. But what about her? What kind of threat did a physical relationship pose to her health? That was the issue here. That was the only issue, he assured himself, refusing to acknowledge feelings that were as foreign as they were unthinkable.

The phone rang again.

He swore under his breath, waited out the call, then raised a brow when she finally said, "It's okay, Dorothy, we'll be right there."

Everything happened at warp speed then, as she disconnected then shoved food back into the refrigerator all the while giving him a hurried explanation of where they had to go and why it had to be right now.

Five

"There." As Lee's truck rolled to a stop, Ellie pointed toward a large pole building about a hundred yards west of the Fergusons' ranch house. "She'll be in that barn."

The phone call had been from their neighbor, Dorothy Ferguson. Don and Dorothy had always been good neighbors. When Ellie had lost her mom, it had been Dorothy who had sat with her in the night and held her while she cried. It had been Don who had watched over Shiloh when her dad had gotten sick and Ellie was dependent on someone to help her with chores and drive her to the hospital to see him and into town for supplies.

Now the Fergusons needed her. She would move heaven and earth to help them.

"Ellie, we're in a fix over here," Dorothy had said, her voice sounding breathless and worried over the phone lines. "Don is down in the back. Doc put him to bed this morning with some muscle relaxants and wouldn't you know it, May Belle picked today to deliver. The fact is, darlin', I'm just no good with birthings. Cal won't be home for his spring break until the end of the month, so I don't have anyone here to help me.

"Gosh, honey, I hate to ask, being you're on your honeymoon and all, but do you suppose I could borrow that beefy bridegroom of yours to help pull the foal? I'm afraid it's comin' breech or it would be over by now. The vet's out of town—something about a convention and the on-call vet is tied up at Chester Gorman's place. It may be hours before he can get here. I really hate this, honey."

Lee had listened to Ellie's urgent but calmly detailed accounting of Dorothy Ferguson's frantic call as he'd buttoned up his shirt. Then he'd snagged his truck keys from the windowsill above the kitchen sink. "I'll be back as soon as I can," he'd said, as the screen door slammed shut behind him.

As bad as he felt about the Fergusons' dilemma, he was suddenly more than grateful for the chance to put a little distance between his libido and his bride.

What little perspective he'd gotten from his hour of slamming steel to wood had gone AWOL when he'd found Ellie in the kitchen, looking luscious and wholesome and, curiously, like she had a burr the size of Texas under her saddle. Even more curious were the violet eyes that had blurred to a cool-blue flame and suggested he might have been the one to put it there.

That had thrown him. That sweet, innocent, dependent little Ellie also had a backbone and a temper that could simmer near flash point had thrown him in spades. It had also excited him and gotten them right back where they'd started when he'd left her in the tub to let off some steam.

Dorothy's call was going to give him the distance he needed before he made another mistake. So he didn't walk, he ran to his truck at a fast jog. When he reached it and realized that Ellie was opening the passenger door at the same time he was crawling in the driver's side, he figured he'd kissed his distance—and his sanity goodbye. That didn't stop him from giving it one last try.

"You don't need to go with me, Ellie," he stated firmly as he jammed the key in the ignition and waited, his hand on the wheel, hoping she would climb out of the cab.

She didn't budge. She buckled herself in, looked straight ahead and said, "Yes, I do," in a deceptively soft voice that fronted a quiet and set determination.

He looked at her over his extended arm, saw the stubborn set of her pixie chin and recognized not only another interesting facet to this woman, but a force to be reckoned with.

It could have been pride in her as much as surprise that sneaked in to undercut his irritation. And he might have smiled at her tenacity if the situation weren't so urgent—and if he hadn't needed some distance from her so badly.

He was supposed to be the voice of experience here. He was supposed to be the one who knew what to do, yet he'd made one mistake after another with her. The first had been in not realizing the extent of her dependence on him because of the epilepsy. The second had been in underestimating the strength of her will.

The most costly error of all, though, had been in letting her totally and completely mess with his head with that little stunt in the tub. He couldn't afford to make any more mistakes where she was concerned because she was the one who was going to suffer if he did.

But since the issue of her staying home or going along to the Fergusons' wasn't a hill he would pick to die on, he slipped the truck in gear and tore out of the drive.

Dorothy was wringing her hands when she walked out onto the porch to greet them.

"Thank goodness you're here! I can't go down there. I just can't stand to see May Belle struggle that way. Besides, it's all I can handle keeping Don in bed. He's bound and determined he's going to crawl down to the barn and help that mare."

"You go take care of Don," Lee heard Ellie say as he rounded the truck and headed for the barn at a trot. "We'll take care of things."

"Ellie, you stay with Dorothy," he ordered over his shoulder—for all the good it did. She was right behind him when he unlatched the barn door and let himself inside.

"I told you to stay with Dorothy." He leveled her his best, take-charge glare. "You don't need to be involved in this." And he didn't need her distracting him. He thought again about that close call with the ax. He'd been thinking about her, seeing her all wet and willing and naked.

It hadn't ended there. He'd just spent fifteen long minutes in his truck at breakneck speed getting over here—had almost lost control at one curve because, instead of concentrating on his driving, he'd been thinking about her. The buoyant softness of her breasts, the inviting resilience of her thighs, the downy copper curls sheltering her virginity.

And she *was* a virgin. He'd been a fool to doubt that. A jealous fool. Everything about her response to his kisses said she was untried, from the sweetness of her sighs to the tentative explorations of her tongue.

He, however, wasn't nineteen anymore, randy as an alley cat and ruled by the pulse below his waist that was raging yet again as he glared down at her. And just kept on glaring because he couldn't seem to take his eyes off her.

A desperate, high-pitched whinny brought his head around and reminded him why he was here. "Please. Go to the house," he said one more time, because he really had to get away from her.

"How long has it been since you pulled a foal?" she asked, sticking to his side as he headed for the back of the barn.

He set his jaw, drew a breath between clenched teeth and, finally resigned to the fact that she wasn't going away, kept on walking. "A while. But I've pulled plenty of calves. It's not that different."

"This is very different." She shouldered past him and unlatched the birthing stall where a big bay mare lay panting and frothed with sweat. "It's different because this is May Belle and she's very special, aren't you girl," she crooned softly as she knelt by the mare's head and soothed her with tender strokes to her jaw.

Another one of those strange, fisting sensations

clutched at his chest as he looked at her there on her knees in the straw.

He made himself look away, check out the situation.

Oh, man. He scrubbed his hand over his jaw. They were in trouble. The mare had lost a lot of blood and, judging by the consistency of the fluid leakage, the umbilical sac may have broken. May Belle's eyes were wild, her breaths rapid. She knew she was in trouble, too. Fatigue and pain showed in the tension in her abdomen and her stiff-legged stretch.

He cupped his nape with a palm, shook his head. Very likely Dorothy's call had come too late.

"No."

He shifted his gaze to Ellie's. The passion of her denial told him that she'd read his thoughts.

"Ellie—"

"We can't lose her. May Belle—May Belle is Don's foundation mare. He's built his breeding program on her babies and her babies' babies. She's Bud's momma," she said, referring to her own chestnut gelding. "We cannot lose her."

Both a child's hopes and a woman's determination fired in her eyes—and kicked an errant Lancelot gene into high gear.

With his gaze fixed on her face, he started rolling up his sleeves. "Talk to her, Ellie. See if you can get her to relax," he suggested softly.

Then he went in search of a bucket of soapy water and prepared for both the physical and mental concentration required to pull, what he hoped, wasn't a dead foal.

Late-afternoon sunlight filtered into the stall. The scent of must and hay and the struggles of life emerging permeated the air and melded with a quiet that had settled over the barn.

"She's so pretty," Ellie whispered as she stood by May Belle's withers and stroked the hip of the still-wet and tentatively nursing filly.

A soft, reassuring nicker and the greedy suckling smacks of the newborn foal having her first meal brought a slow smile to her face.

For the past fifteen minutes Lee had sat quietly in the corner of the stall, watching Ellie, watching the foal, rubbing the circulation back into his right arm. And brooding. He was getting damned good at that.

A stray beam of sunlight flitted around her curls and set them afire. He wanted to wrap a fiery gold curl around his finger, fist his hand in the heavy silk of her hair, draw her to him, feel his hands on her skin, fill her as a woman can only be filled by a man.

He let out a deep breath, let his head fall back against the wall of the stall.

What are you doing to me, Ellie?

She drew feelings from him—anger, desperation, longing—that he had never let himself feel. He'd had little time for emotion in his life to this point, less need. And now...now he couldn't think for the havoc she was wreaking. He didn't like it, but he couldn't muster up enough resistance to shove it all out of the way. It was starting to wear on him.

"Your arm? Is it getting any better?"

Her soft voice brought his head up. He blinked, willed the sexual haze to lift. "The good news? The feeling's back. The bad news? The feeling's back."

She smiled. "It hurts bad, huh?"

He shook his head. "It's fine."

It wasn't fine, and he'd been stupid. They both knew it—she was just kind enough not to point it out.

He'd made a mistake. Big surprise. He'd been on his knees in the straw behind the laboring mare and reached in to try to turn the foal. It was standard operating procedure. The trick was timing. Never enter a birth canal until after a contraction. He'd been so entranced by the look of his bride as she'd sweet-talked and whispered and murmured tender encouragement to a thousand pounds of laboring horseflesh, that he'd lost sight of anything but her.

When May Belle had gone into a full contraction, he'd been in shoulder deep. Idiotic move. Painful move. Only luck had kept him from ending up with a dislocated shoulder or a broken arm. Just like it was only luck that both mare and foal had pulled through.

"They're going to be okay, aren't they?" She left the bonding pair and walked to his side, looking down on him.

He let out a deep breath, still baffled. "They shouldn't have made it. Neither one of them. But, yeah, they're going to be just fine."

He'd given them up for lost the minute he'd sized up the situation. Ellie hadn't let him get away with it. He could tell that she wanted to give him credit, but if anyone was responsible, she was—just as she was responsible for a lot of things he didn't understand and didn't want to deal with right now.

Determined not to, he rolled wearily to his hip, then his knees and started to stand.

Her hand reached down for his. He hesitated for a moment, then grasped it.

Her hand was small, but there was strength in her

grip. It shouldn't have surprised him—but then, why not. Just about everything about her did.

He let her help him to his feet—and then stood there, holding on to her hand, searching her eyes.

How did you get so strong, Ellie? he wondered. How do you stand so strong with all you have to deal with?

"Thanks," he croaked around the lump that had suddenly lodged in his throat. And then he couldn't help it. He pulled her into his arms, tucked her head under his chin and thought of a hundred things he wanted to say to her. But that would require some disclosure on his part. He wasn't even close to wanting to deal with that—or with the truths he might reveal if he did start talking.

So what came out was, "I'm a mess."

He squeezed her hard and because his overriding need was to keep her there, set her away. "Come on. Let's go tell Dorothy the good news. Then let's go home."

Home.

He drove back to Shiloh in silence, trying not to think about how quickly he'd come to associate the word with the woman who sat by his side.

A sliver of lavender, deep purple and shimmering silver was all that was left of the sunset when Ellie watched Lee walk into the kitchen, fresh from his shower.

They'd been back from the Fergusons' for a little more than an hour. She was determined to talk to him, and while he'd showered, she'd put all the words in place, lined them up like soldiers, steady, strong, direct. But then she saw him. Her mouth went bone dry and the words…the words got lost somewhere between her scattered heartbeats.

He was barefoot, his clean jeans riding low on his hips; the tails of his worn chambray shirt hung loose, the buttons were undone. The forest-green towel he held in his hands was damp. So was his hair. Thick and dark, it curled softly at his nape, even as he worked it ruthlessly with the towel, brushing it back from his forehead.

He was so handsome it made her chest hurt. And his blue eyes were so distant and closed off it made her stomach knot.

"You go ahead and shower," he'd insisted when they pulled into the drive. "I'll do chores."

So she had. She'd showered and thought and then she'd waited in the kitchen, set out their dinner that had turned into supper and rehearsed what she was going to say the minute he came downstairs.

Now here he stood, and all she could do was ache at the look of him. And feel the chill.

They'd shared something special in that barn with May Belle and her baby. Ellie couldn't name it, but she recognized the subtle difference just the same. She'd thought they had turned a corner—only now it looked as if they'd lost their way again in the lonesome silence on the drive home.

He'd been fighting mad when he'd found her in the kitchen earlier. For that matter, so had she been. She'd been ready to tell him a thing or two about frogs and princes and how she wasn't so sure she hadn't ended up with the green one of the two.

She understood now where her anger had come from. She'd been conditioned to always be on the defensive. Past experience had taught her it was the

best protection from curious stares and taunting re-
marks. But Lee wasn't like that. He'd never been like
that. He didn't see her as an oddity, and she was
ashamed that she'd sold him short—even if she'd had
provocation.

But now she was dealing with something else
again. Something that made her want to shout, "Talk
to me. Tell me what I'm doing wrong."

Instead she watched him snag a drumstick as he
headed for the fridge, where he searched inside until
he found the milk.

"You must be starving."

Great. All those words she'd rehearsed and that's
what came out. She'd lost her courage now that she
was face-to-face with him again. Her insecurities took
over just like that, much stronger than she was.

What if he simply didn't want to be with her? What
if there had been another woman in his life in Texas?
A woman he had left because he'd promised her
daddy he'd take care of her.

A woman. Not a girl with a problem.

Suddenly she didn't want to know.

So instead of facing her demons, she followed his
lead and walked to the cupboard and got him a glass.

He made a humming sound around the chicken leg,
which passed for appreciation that he was finally getting something in his stomach.

"Good," he managed after swallowing a healthy
mouthful and washing it down with milk she'd poured
for him. "Nothing better than cold fried chicken.
You're a good cook, Ellie," he added after helping
himself to the potato salad and a homemade bun.

"I had a good teacher."

The wave of sorrow that swamped her was as powerful as it was unexpected. So were the sudden tears she tried like crazy to blink back. She quickly turned her back to him and stared out the kitchen window.

I miss you, Momma. I miss you, Daddy. I need you. Both of you, to tell me how to be a wife. I don't know what to do. I don't know how to reach him—or if he even wants me to. If he even wants me.

"Ellie."

She felt him at her back, his heat, his strength, and because it was what she needed most, she turned into the arms that opened to her.

Then she held on. Just held on as his heart beat strong and sure beneath her cheek. "I miss them," she confessed against his shirt.

"I know, baby." His arms banded tighter around her. "I miss them, too."

She pressed her face into the warmth of his throat. "I'm sorry. I didn't mean to do this." She clutched at the soft cotton shirt that smelled of him and of soap. "Sometimes…sometimes it just sneaks up on me. And I feel so alone."

He rocked her gently back and forth. "You're not alone anymore," he whispered, and pressed a kiss to the top of her head.

"Come on." He set her gently away. "You're tired. And you need to eat as much as I do."

So they ate. In a fractured silence filled with carefully guarded smiles and little else.

He helped her do the dishes.

Then they went to bed.

At least she did.

With her heart in her throat, she waited for him to join her. But he never did.

Not that night. Or any night in the week that followed.

Each morning he would greet her with a smile, a careful distant peck on her cheek and a "How are you?" that was quickly followed by "I'll see you later, then, if you're sure you're okay." Then he'd take off fixing this and fixing that as if there wasn't going to be a tomorrow—or as if he didn't want to spend any time alone with her.

Ellie would feed her birds. She would water her seedlings and plan her garden, cook his meals, wash his clothes and wonder what to do.

Each night in the dark, in her bed, she would close her eyes and wish that it was Lee who was with her—instead of just his words that played like an echo in her mind.

You're not alone anymore.

But she was.

She was alone and she wished with all her heart that she were woman enough to make him understand.

Every day, along with the mail, Leon Wilks brought the daily edition of the *Wall Street Journal* and the *Denver Post*.

Every night after supper Lee snagged them like they were lifelines and went out to the porch to read each one from cover to cover.

They'd developed a pattern. It was working, he told himself.

Yeah, right. That's why he averaged two hours of sleep a night on the couch because he didn't dare use one of the bedrooms upstairs that was so close to hers.

And it was why Ellie looked so lost.

He'd hurt her.

When he left her alone in her room each night, he hurt her. He knew it. He just couldn't get past it.

He told himself it was because he was giving her time. In truth, he was the one who needed the time. He really didn't know how to handle this. Any of it. Not his physical desire for her that had become a matter of pride that he control. Not his inability to figure out how to approach the subject of her epilepsy.

In that moment last Sunday when he'd held her and she'd cried for her parents, it had hit home again just how young she was. How fragile. And he'd known he had to back off until he could get a grip.

For all the good that idea had done him. He was as owly as a bear with beestings. And he was restless. As restless as she was.

From the porch he could hear her in the house, setting the kitchen right after supper, tidying up the dining room.

They couldn't go on like this. Something had to change. He just wished that he knew how or where to go from here. Folding the papers, he pulled off his reading glasses and set them both aside. Rocking forward in the ancient and creaking wicker chair, he tried to think things through—then frowned at the lane leading to Shiloh.

"What the hell?"

He stood up, walked to the end of the new porch floor just as Ellie came outside, her brows furrowed, a dish towel forgotten in her hand. She'd seen it, too—or heard it.

A long line of what—with a little fanciful imagination—looked like a ribbon of fireflies, trailed down the road. In reality it was a string of headlights cutting through the darkening dusk.

There must have been close to twenty cars and pickups, and they were all blowing their horns non-stop.

"Something's wrong," he said as he headed for the bottom step with Ellie right behind him.

They stood there, prepared for the worst, when one by one the vehicles pulled up in front of the house and killed the horns. The loudest cacophony of clang-ing and banging and hoots and hollers and laughter erupted then as dozens of people spilled out into the night beating on pots and pans that they carried like drums.

Lee shot Ellie a baffled look.

She just lifted her shoulders, as befuddled as he was, until the wrinkled old face of Buzz Sheppard grinned up at them from the bottom of the steps.

"Shivaree!" Buzz shouted gleefully and, pounding a wooden spoon on the bottom of a blackened old stew pot, led the laughing throng around the house in a shuffling dance that only they knew the steps to. "Shivaree! Shivaree!"

"Shiva-what?" Lee shouted above the noise, bend-ing his head close to hers.

Ellie smiled then, and a laugh bubbled out as the howling, pan-banging parade passed by.

"Shivaree," she shouted, then clasped her hands together as warmth filled her chest. "They're giving us a shivaree."

"What the hell is a shivaree?" He placed an arm over her shoulders and drew her against his side.

"It's a noisy mock serenade to newlyweds," she

explained, tipping her head up to his so he could hear her. "It's an old Sundown custom."

A mock serenade to a mock marriage. The irony hit him where it hurt—and where he knew it must hurt Ellie.

But she was smiling, and for her sake he put on his game face.

"An old custom and a loud one," he said with a forced laugh, then waved when he recognized Pastor Good and his wife, Martha. "Does this mean I have to share your leftover pot roast with them?"

Her eyes were shining. "Something tells me they're going to be sharing a lot more with us than we are with them."

The noisy bunch rounded the house about that time and headed back for their vehicles. When they trooped back up the walk, the only noise was their laughing chatter. Buzz had traded his stew pot and spoon for a fiddle. Someone brought out a guitar. Everyone else carried covered casseroles, bowls of salad and armloads of prettily wrapped packages. There was even a wedding cake—compliments of Doc Lundstrum's wife.

Lee wanted to be annoyed. He was frustrated. He was concerned about Ellie. But when he looked down and saw her smiling face, he couldn't be anything but happy for her.

He simply stepped aside as their unexpected guests trooped inside and took over.

Six

"**H**e watches you." Peg Lathrop lifted a forkful of wedding cake and grinned at Ellie.

Ellie blinked, then looked at the young woman who had sought her out where she'd sat in the corner of the living room surrounded by wrapping paper and the wedding gifts she and Lee had recently opened.

When Peg laughed at Ellie's look of disbelief, Ellie searched for Lee. She found him standing in the arched doorway that separated the living room from the dining room. He *was* watching her, but he quickly looked away and returned his attention to Dorothy Ferguson, who had arrived with a slow-moving Don in tow.

"Can't keep his eyes off you," Peg added knowingly when Ellie met her gaze again.

"Um," was all Ellie could manage as she looked from Peg to Lee again.

He looked so tall and lean, so confident and strong as he laughed at something Dorothy said, his white teeth flashing, the creases around his eyes and mouth deepening.

She thought about that mouth, about the way it had felt on hers the day of their wedding, the morning after in her bed and later in the tub. She thought about it when she washed dishes or when she was gathering eggs. She thought about it each night, as she lay alone in her bed.

Peg touched her arm, smiling softly. "So I take it the feeling's mutual?"

The pair of embroidered pillowcases Martha Good had given them as a wedding gift suddenly became the focus of her attention. She wanted desperately to confide in Peg. She had always been one of Ellie's most special alliances. Peg was twenty-six and a single mom. In Sundown, Montana, population 473, that alone was a pretty big cross to bear. Ellie hadn't cared about any of that. She liked Peg, who had always made it a point to talk to Ellie when they'd run into each other at church, or at Lathrop Feed Store where Peg kept books for her dad.

Unlike most people close to her age, the epilepsy didn't bother Peg. For the most part those same people ignored her or stared with either a warped sort of fascination or a guilt-ridden pity. Peg was different. Peg accepted her for who she was. And for that alone, Peg, with her flashing brown eyes and long slim body, would always be special to Ellie.

"Well," Peg prompted with a gentle elbow in Ellie's ribs, "How's it goin'?"

Ellie felt the blush all the way to her toes.

Peg laughed. "That good, huh?" But her smile

faded as she took a second look at Ellie's face and didn't like what she saw. "Uh-oh. What's wrong?"

Even though Ellie was a private person, with Peg she didn't feel so guarded. The words were out before she knew it. "I wish I knew."

Wisely Peg didn't say anything. She simply waited.

"I'm not so sure he's all that happy about...about being saddled with me," Ellie finally admitted.

She ran a thumbnail along the intricately embroidered stitches that made a purple iris and a yellow crocus on the pillowslip and dodged Peg's probing gaze.

"Oh, honey." Peg grasped her hands, glared over at Lee, then relaxed when she saw he was watching Ellie with a quietly predatory look, and with a hunger that even Peg—who had been in dry dock for longer than she cared to admit—recognized for what it was. "I don't think for a minute that's the problem. When he looks at you, there's enough heat in that man's eyes to fire a furnace."

"Then why am I still a virgin almost a week after my wedding?" Ellie blurted out in a whisper.

Peg blinked. Ellie watched her blink again before she added a quiet, "Oh."

Ellie spilled it all then. She'd needed someone to talk to for so long. Peg listened with quiet encouragement while Ellie told her about the seizure on her wedding day, about Lee holding her all night that night, about what had happened in the bathtub, and about every night she'd slept alone in her bed since.

"Come on," Peg said, after a moment. She stood and tugged Ellie out onto the porch. "I think I know what's going on here but, just to make sure, tell me everything again. And don't leave one thing out."

* * *

Later that night Lee sat alone in the big wicker rocker on the shadowed porch. Storm clouds had ruled the morning but had given way by midday to full sun. Now, close to 1:00 a.m.—an hour since the shivaree had ended and the last old dog had packed up his pots and pans and tottered home—thunderheads were stacking up again. An egg-shaped moon winked in and out of the clouds that scudded across the sky like a troop of slowly patrolling night watchmen.

He leaned forward, propped his elbows on his knees and stared at his loosely clasped hands as a night breeze picked up and sent Ellie's wind chimes dancing.

She had been exhausted by the time the crowd had left. Exhausted and happier than he'd been able to make her since he'd come back to Shiloh and married her.

In spite of himself he had to smile when he thought of the gathered throng. Old Doc, Buzz and a couple of dozen others. His smile faded to a frown. One person. There had been only one person in on the shivaree who was even close to Ellie's age.

It told him too much about Ellie's life that Peg Lathrop was the only young person from Sundown in the group. Where were the friends her own age?

Even as he formed the thought, he knew the answer. There weren't any. These were her parents' friends. These were the people of Sundown who cared about her. These were the ones she trusted to accept her as she was.

He leaned back again, listened to the muffled creak of the rocker and the chirp of spring's first crickets in the grass around the lattice-wrapped porch. In the far distance a low roll of thunder rumbled across the mountain ridge. In the not-so-far distance rumbled the grim reminder of how cruel kids could be.

He'd had his own mechanisms in place back then for dealing with the taunts that had labeled him everything from ''outsider'' to ''loser'' to ''welfare case.'' He'd knocked the snot out of anyone who'd even looked at him sideways. He raised a hand, rubbed a finger over the small crescent-shaped scar at the corner of his mouth. That scar, along with the slight bend in his nose that hadn't set quite right after it had been broken by a fist in the face were reminders of those angry, defensive fights he'd been quick to start and slow to walk away from. While his anger hadn't changed anyone's view of him, or for that matter, his view of himself, his choice of expressing it had shut them up. And, right or wrong, it had given him an outlet for his rage and humiliation.

You didn't have that option, did you, Ellie?

At a level that he'd hadn't let himself fully acknowledge since returning to Shiloh, he understood that he didn't hold the only advanced degree from the school of hard knocks. He'd grown up on the streets, been kicked around, left to twist in the wind and fend for himself until Will and Clare had found him.

Ellie was a graduate of that school, too, except she'd had a different set of classes to deal with. With her illness came so many limitations, so much disappointment. So many reasons not to trust and so much time alone. And so many reasons to be bitter and disillusioned and swayed to the side of defeat.

Yet look at her. She was none of those things.

He drew in a deep breath. Let it out. And wished he'd been around to slay her dragons for her.

Well, he was here to take care of her now. And he'd been right to leave her alone each night. It was for her good, not his.

Walking away from her bed each night had nothing to do with wanting her so badly it consumed him. Walking away had nothing to do with a creeping, seeping suspicion that if there was a need here, it was the one he felt to be surrounded by her goodness, to draw from her strength, to open himself up to feelings that he'd spent his entire life convincing himself didn't exist—or that he, at least, had control over.

That control went on red alert when he heard the front door open, then close.

He stiffened when she walked past him on bare feet. With her back to him, she leaned against the porch rail to watch the shifting shades of gray cloud creep across the moon and douse the light.

"You couldn't sleep, either?" Her voice was as soft as the night breeze that tugged at her hair that hung nearly to her waist. The tumble of curls looked as soft as she looked bewitching.

He swallowed hard as a break in the cloud cover flooded moonlight across his bride and the white-on-white nightgown she wore.

Where was her robe, he thought frantically? Where was her fussy pink robe that covered her from ankle to throat and only gave him glimpses and guesses at the curves that lay beneath?

Where did she get that…that whisper of a gown that left nothing and everything to the imagination? Virginal white. Long and flowing. As gossamer as sea mist, as concealing as a bridal veil. Her back was still to him, and he could see every curve and contour of her womanly body. The soft flair of her hips, the rounded firmness of her buttocks, the slim line of her legs.

He tried to look away; he couldn't. And he knew in that moment he was in very large trouble.

"I like to come out here, too, when I'm having trouble sleeping." She turned to him then and pressed her cheek to a porch post that he'd painted two days ago. When he was sane. Which he wasn't now. Which he had no hope of becoming as she hugged the post with her arm and leaned against it.

"I guess I shouldn't have had that last cup of coffee," he croaked, unable to take his eyes off her, which only got him into more trouble.

It was a honeymoon gown, he realized finally. Very sheer. Very flowing. Very—he suppressed a groan— very sexy.

The hem skimmed the floor, though the toes of her tiny bare feet peeked out beneath it. The neckline was round and low, held together between her breasts with a single delicate white satin ribbon. He could see the shadowed outline of her nipples pressing against the softly clinging fabric that the night breeze molded against her sweet, sweet breasts. Against her flat belly and the slight indentation of her navel. The downy curls at the apex of her thighs.

"You." He cleared his throat, tried again while his heart jumped into a jungle beat. "You should go back inside. You—" He swallowed as her nipples tightened then pressed like diamonds against silk. "You must be...cold."

And he was hot. Blistering hot and already imagining that with one flick of his finger he could undo the ribbon that held her gown in place. With one tug of his hand he could peel that skim of material from her breast and feel the velvet softness of her nipple against his tongue. Taste the silk of her skin. Draw her deep into his mouth.

"Do you want me to go inside, Lee?" She took a slow step toward him.

He groaned, closed his eyes...and opened them to find her kneeling at his feet...searching his face with eyes the color of summer violets...covering his thighs with small, warm hands—hands that he'd imagined touching him in places that would shock her and send him straight over the edge.

"Ellie." It was a serrated, grating whisper that begged her to leave before he forgot why he was still clinging to a desperate notion that he was saving her from whatever the hell he was so certain he needed to save her from.

He clamped his fingers around the arms of the rocker to keep from reaching for her. To keep from ravaging her. "Go to bed," he ordered gruffly.

"I've been to bed," she whispered as she rose and eased onto his lap.

He swallowed hard, dug deep and found very little to hang on to—except her. She looped one arm around his neck, pressed the palm of her other hand against his chest where his heart slammed like a jackhammer. She smelled like vanilla and cinnamon and woman.

"I've been to bed," she repeated softly. "It was lonely there. It's *been* lonely there."

It was too much. He was only human. And she was his wife. Her scent surrounded him, her slight weight, the heavy curtain of her hair, teased by the wind, fluttered across his face, snagged on his midnight stubble.

He wanted everything she offered. He craved it. And as she shifted so she could look into his eyes, and inadvertently pressed her hip against the rock-hard length of his arousal, he thought he'd die if he couldn't take it.

"Don't you want me, Lee?"

Moonlight danced across her fiery curls and cast her face in shadow.

"Don't want you?" He groaned, incredulous, and surrendered…to the night that tempered his sanity, to the eyes that begged him to love her, to the need that had grown beyond denial.

"I have wanted you…" His hands moved to span her waist and settle her hips deeper into his lap. "I have wanted you for what seems like forever."

He skated a hand up her ribs then across one sweet breast and higher, to span his fingers along her throat and tip her face to his. "Your mouth. Ellie—" he brushed his thumb across her lower lip, felt her tremble "—how I've wanted your mouth."

Ellie caught her breath, bit back a moan as a wild, delicious arc of heat shot from her breast to her belly where it pooled, then spread like liquid fire.

Peg had been right. He *did* want her. And she'd been a fool to wonder and worry and not take matters into her own hands. The problem, she realized now, was not that he saw her as different, not that he didn't want her, but that he didn't want to see her as a woman. He wanted to think of her as his charge—or thought he *should* think of her that way. That much Peg had helped her figure out. She just wasn't sure why he was so determined on the issue.

Determined or not, he was seeing her differently now.

He'd started seeing her differently, she realized, that morning when he'd kissed her in the bathtub. She wasn't sure why she knew—maybe it was that woman's intuition Momma had always talked about—but she understood now that in that moment he'd not only seen her as a woman, he'd wanted her as one. And he hadn't been very happy with himself because of it.

The *why* of it still puzzled her. The *how* of getting him past it, however, was starting to become very clear. To make him treat her like a woman, she simply had to behave like one.

"Will you kiss me, Lee? Will...will you kiss me like you did that morning in the bathtub?"

She barely got the last word out before he lowered his head and covered her mouth with his.

And kissed her. The way a man is supposed to kiss a woman, she thought, as she threw her arms around his neck and hung on, ready to go anywhere he wanted to take her.

"Oh. Oh," she murmured on a breathless sigh when he tilted his head to increase the contact, adjust the angle, heighten the pleasure. And there was pleasure. So much, so fast, her heart was racing as she turned into him, wanting, suddenly, to crawl under his skin and be a part of him from the inside out.

"Ellie...Ellie, sweetheart."

From a distance she heard him whisper her name. With a small whimper of protest she felt his mouth leave hers, only to slam back hard for a fierce, hungry kiss before he dragged his mouth away again.

"Lee."

"Shush, baby."

A warm hand cupped her cheek as he pressed his lips to her forehead and drew in a ragged breath. "I'm not going anywhere. I'm just…just slowing things down a little."

"I liked it fast."

A harsh laugh rumbled against her breast. "Oh, I know. I know you did. But…just trust me on this, okay? You're gonna like it this way, too."

"What way?" she felt dazed as she lay back in his arms and watched his face, watched his eyes go dark and hazy.

"Slow and easy," he whispered, and good to his word, eased his hand slowly down her cheek, along the column of her throat. "Very, very slow. Very, very easy."

She was breathless with anticipation as, in agonizingly slow motion, his hand stole lower to finally cup and caress her breast through her gown. Everything inside her clenched at the wondrous pleasure, at the electric thrill of his hand touching her where she had longed for him to touch her for what seemed like forever.

She closed her eyes, arched into his hand as he caressed and stroked, then circled her nipple with the tip of his thumbnail.

"Oh." Stunning sensations spiraled through her body. She wanted them to go on forever, yet she wanted more. "Lee."

"Shush. Easy, remember? Let me go slow and easy with you, Ellie. We've both waited so long."

She opened her eyes, her trust complete, her need enveloping her in a new set of feelings, a new sense of awareness.

He lifted her then, shifted her until she was no longer lying sideways in his arms but straddling his lap. Her knees pressed into the flowered cushion on either side of his hips, her gown bunched around her thighs in silky folds. Her bottom nestled on his muscled thighs and he very purposefully lifted her arms and draped them over his shoulders as her hair drifted over hers. He clasped his hands at her hips and held her there, warm against him, open against him.

It was shocking. Exciting. She'd never felt more vulnerable, or more alive.

"Kiss me, Ellie." His blue eyes were dark with promise, his voice, a velvet command. "Kiss me the way you've been wanting to kiss me."

She searched his face, then studied his mouth, the full lower lip, the lovely cupid's bow of his upper lip, the tiny scar that resembled a crescent moon. She wasn't aware that she had licked her own lips, savoring the feast to come. When his mouth curved up in an indulgent smile, she realized what she'd done and felt her face flush in the moonlight.

"It's all right." He turned his face to the inside of her forearm, bit her gently, then kissed the tender flesh in supplication. "I love how you look at me."

"How do I look at you?" Her voice sounded breathless, just the way she felt as he turned back to her, his cobalt-blue gaze drifting across her face beneath the sweep of dark thick lashes.

"Like you want to eat me up in little bites."

It was her turn to smile as a newfound confidence bolstered her. "I'd rather have a big bite, please."

He laughed, and the sound filled her with love and desire and a confidence she'd never dreamed she had in her. She leaned forward, touched her mouth softly to his.

He drew in a breath, closed his eyes. And she smiled and, still smiling, touched her mouth to his again. This time she lingered and licked and learned the shape of him, and understood that she fed his hunger when his arms banded around her and he dragged her hard against him.

She loved his tongue. The taste of it, the bold possession as it swept inside her mouth and claimed, then teased, then gentled until she was the one teasing and he was the one squirming to draw her closer, he was the one fighting for a steady breath.

"Umm." She licked her lips as she pulled away and sat back down on his thighs. "You taste like coffee. And wedding cake."

"And you taste...Ellie, you taste like heaven." His gaze on hers, he skimmed his hands up ribs and stopped, just below her breasts. Ever so softly he brushed his thumbs up and along the tips of her nipples.

She shivered and tried not to whimper.

"Can I taste you here?" he asked quietly, making it clear with the steady sweep of his thumbs where he wanted his mouth, what he wanted to do.

She'd read the book. She'd seen the pictures. She'd imagined what it would feel like to have Lee's mouth on her breasts. To feel him kiss her there. But she'd seen pictures of a man's hands on a woman's breasts, too, and she'd imagined what that would feel like. Imagination hadn't begun to compare to reality. So just thinking of Lee's mouth there, where his hands had been, sent a lush, liquid heat gushing through her body.

"Yes, oh, yes," she answered, and with flying fingers reached for the ribbon that held her gown closed.

His hands stilled hers. She looked up, watched him through a curtain of hair.

He brushed it back from her face, tucked it behind her ear. "First like this." With his hands spanning her waist, he lifted her until she was standing on her knees before him.

Her breasts were on a level with his mouth. She could feel the tips tighten just thinking about what he would do next. And what he did next made her draw in her breath and dig her fingers into his shoulders.

He urged her forward with those big, gentle hands on her waist and breathed on her. A warm breath, a gentle caress, a promise that made her shiver and burn all at the same time.

"More?" He bussed his nose around the edge of her aureole.

She did whimper then, and pressed herself against him.

"Definitely more," he murmured with a smile in his voice as he kissed the valley between her breasts, then worked his way in small, eating kisses to the peak of her left nipple.

She clutched a handful of his hair, sighed his name.

And then he surrounded her, biting her lightly through her gown, driving her wild with the wet sweep of his tongue against fabric and skin, making her moan, making her yearn. He tasted his fill, lingering over one breast, then the other until he finally pulled away and with his eyes gone slumberous and dark, gave her permission to undo her gown.

Her fingers were shaking as she untied the small ribbon. Her breath was shallow, as shimmering silk fell open, exposing a pale slice of flesh to the night and to his eyes. His hands moved slowly, first to cover her, then to caress, then to separate silk from skin. Slower still, he brushed the gown aside. Her heart was in her throat as she shrugged it off her shoulders, then lifting her arms, let it slide free to pool at her hips.

She watched him swallow, felt his fingers spread wide beneath her shoulder blades as he looked his fill, murmured his approval, then pulled her unerringly toward him.

It could have been her name she heard escape his lips, it could have been a prayer. She didn't know. Didn't care, couldn't think for the feel of his mouth on her skin. Naked lips to naked breast.

She had never imagined. Had never known about the magic, the magnitude of sensations. A man's mouth. Lee's mouth, drawing on her breast. The stubble of his cheek brushing her skin, the heat of his breath. It was more than a delicious, mind-numbing sensation, it was a deep, soul-deep communion. And she understood in that wonderful moment that she wasn't the only one who needed this physical contact. *He* needed. He needed her. She felt it with the gentleness of his touch, the endless depth of his hunger.

His eyes were deep, dark extensions of his soul as he kissed her breast one last time, then slumped back in the chair, watching her. Wanting her. His gaze never left her face as he ran his hand up and under flowing silk that drifted across her thighs. He spread his fingers wide, absorbing the resilience of her muscles beneath his palms, the warmth of her flesh.

His gaze locked on hers, he slid his hands slowly toward her center.

"Can I touch you here?" His voice was a scratchy, velvet whisper.

She shivered, felt her inner muscles clench, felt herself pulse and swell—and for the first time felt a twinge of self-consciousness. But this was Lee. This was her husband whose lap she straddled, her husband whose gaze had gone smoky and dark, her husband whose mouth had suckled her breasts and wanted to touch her intimately. This, finally, was her lover.

The night breeze lifted her hair, whispered across her breasts still wet from his loving, still tight with longing.

She leaned forward, brushed his lips with hers. "Please," she murmured into the warm, wet wonder that was his mouth as his hands moved higher up her thighs, his thumb stroking, enticing, "Please, please touch me. Touch me there."

She watched his eyes as he brushed the back of his knuckles against her curls. She breathed his name, waiting, waiting for the touch of him. For the love of him.

He touched her then.

Finally.

Gently.

Then deeply.

She heard herself moan, felt her fingers dig into his shoulders and didn't care that she was completely open, totally vulnerable. It felt so...exotic and so unexpectedly shocking. So extraordinarily good.

With a light hand he stroked her, a delicious little swirl of his finger to her core. She felt her own wetness, thought she should be embarrassed by it but was too lost in sensation to do anything but hold him tighter and wish she knew how to ask for more.

Somehow he knew. He gave more without her asking, intensifying the pressure, increasing the speed until she rocked involuntarily against his touch, begging him for something…something. She didn't know. She just wanted it to go on and on, this pleasure that was so pure and so perfect that she gave herself over to it. Lost herself in the wonder as it built to an electric, enveloping climax that eclipsed thought, vanquished control and ripped through her body like a starburst. With a shattered cry she let it take her, let it toss her, let it consume her until she collapsed against him, boneless and winded and deliriously devastated.

Lee gathered her against him, his heart pounding in tandem with hers. He wanted—more than he wanted his next breath—he wanted to free himself from his jeans and bury himself deep inside her. He was past denying that he wanted her—all she'd had to do was ask. All she'd had to do was offer, and all of his resolve had folded like a tower of precariously stacked cards.

She'd held the trump card tonight. In retrospect he realized now that she always had. He'd just been fooling himself into believing he was the one who would call the shots and make the rules.

He knotted a fist in her hair, absorbed her heat and the aftershocks that rippled through her delicate, hot little body. Her first time. He'd been amazed by her responses. He'd expected hesitation. He'd expected shyness. And yes, there had been some. It had flickered across her face just as the moonlight had flickered through the clouds, but she'd quickly denied it and leaped without fear into his arms. Into his soul, with her breathless sighs, her fearless heart.

Addiction. He'd never understood it. He thought he might have a loose handle on it now. He could get addicted to the look of her, the feel of her, the scent of her coming apart in his arms.

She shivered and snuggled closer, her breathing leveling, her heartbeat settling. She was so limp, so…wasted…he tempered his desire, dived headlong into concern—where he should have been from the moment she'd walked into the moonlight and stolen his breath and his sanity.

Too much. He'd taken too much. He'd pressed her too soon.

"Ellie? Sweetheart?"

She sighed and wrapped herself around him as if he was a bed and she wanted to cover him like a satin sheet.

He stroked a hand over her hair. And did what was essential that he do. He catered to her needs and put his on hold.

"Let's get you to bed before you catch a chill," he whispered, and, shifting her in his arms rose and carried her into the house and up the stairs, the gown that was tangled around her hips trailing them like a shadow.

She was asleep before he laid her down on her white-on-white bed, where the covers were thrown back, where the sweet indentation of her body lingered on both the sheets and her pillow. He didn't know whether to feel smug or cheated.

What he absolutely did feel was protective as he leaned over her and simply looked at her—the wild tangle of copper-gold curls trailing across the pillow, her pale, slim body languidly sated, her rose-pink nipples soft as velvet now.

She'd come apart for him. Eager and proud, curious and brave. The punch of desire hit him again. This time he was prepared for it. He'd had a week of practice. A week of holding back, holding off. He could go another night. Or as many as it took to make sure she was ready for him.

He couldn't wait to take her up again, then take her down with him. But not tonight. Not as exhausted as she was. He knew that he hadn't gotten much sleep the last week. He seriously doubted that she had, either.

So he bit back the need, curbed the desire. He looked longingly at the bed, at his beautiful sleeping wife, and knew that if he joined her there, he wouldn't be able to leave her alone.

Tomorrow, he promised himself as he headed back downstairs to his bed on the sofa. Tomorrow they would talk. Tomorrow he would know what their future held.

Tomorrow he might even come up with an explanation for this indescribable warmth that clotted his chest when he looked at her and made him want to believe that maybe he'd been wrong. Maybe Sara had been wrong.

Maybe…just maybe, he had the capability of being something more to a woman than just there.

Seven

Ellie had been awake since sunup. She'd lain in her bed and tried to make sense of why Lee wasn't with her. It had been incredible. Out on the porch, when he'd kissed her, and touched her. It had been so…wonderful.

And then he'd left her. Asleep in her bed. Alone again.

When all of her reasoning pointed back in the same direction, she swallowed her pride, got dressed for church and went downstairs.

She'd already fried the bacon and the pancake batter was ready for the griddle when she heard him walk softly into the kitchen. She tried not to stiffen. Tried not to let the hurt show. But he must have sensed it, anyway.

"Ellie?"

His voice was soft behind her. She lowered her

head, then immediately lifted her chin and reached for the bowl of batter. She would not let him see her humiliation.

"Good morning," she said brightly, and shot a quick smile over her shoulder.

That was a mistake. He was all sleep rumpled— pillow creases dented his stubbled cheek, and his hair was beautifully mussed. His shirt hung open; his feet were bare. Seeing him that way, still warm from his bed on the couch when he should have been warm from her bed, was a grim reminder of how much of him she didn't have, how much she might never have.

She closed her mind to the picture and its message. "I thought you were going to sleep all morning. Church isn't for a couple of hours yet so I made pancakes. I can scramble some eggs if—"

"Ellie." His hand on her shoulders stopped her forced, cheery banter. "Look at me."

She didn't want to look at him. Didn't want to see the pity or regret or distaste or whatever it was he was feeling this morning. But she forced herself. She pasted on a smile, met his dark scowl.

And waited with her heart in her throat.

"Ellie, what's wrong?"

"Nothing. Nothing's wrong."

"You feeling okay?"

"I feel fine."

A long moment passed. "But you're upset," he finally decided.

She drew a bracing breath. "I'm not upset. Why would I be upset?" She heard the bite in her reply. Was sorry she hadn't been able to curb it. Or maybe not. Maybe she didn't just want to roll over and play the I'm-fine-don't-concern-yourself-with-me game.

Maybe she wanted to hurt him, the way he had hurt her.

"Why would I be upset?" she repeated, letting loose with some of the fire that had been building in her belly. Let him see what he'd done to her. Let him deal with it.

Lee watched her warily. He'd expected that she might feel self-conscious this morning. He'd expected she might feel shy. He hadn't expected anger. And she was angry. Beyond angry.

He walked to the cupboard, snagged a mug from the shelf and poured a cup of coffee. He needed a hit of caffeine to help clear his head. He hadn't slept much last night. He glanced at her. At her fever-bright eyes that were agitated and narrowed in accusation and in complete contrast to the serene pastels of her pretty flowing dress that made him think of her flower garden of a bedroom.

He figured that he knew what this was all about. He'd made another major mistake last night. He'd known it then, was sure of it now. He should have trusted his instincts. He should have walked away from her before...well, by the looks of her, before he'd taken her somewhere she wasn't prepared to go, let alone to deal with in the cool clear light of morning.

"I'm sorry," he said finally. When she just glared at him, her eyes filled with hurt and anger and a humiliation that he'd put there, he set aside the coffee and went to her.

"Don't. Don't touch me." She threw her arms wide, bolting away from his outstretched arms. "Don't touch me like I'm something that will break."

He stopped in his tracks, suddenly confused. He

was low enough on sleep and high enough on sexual frustration that a healthy bite of anger of his own shot out before he could rein it in. "I don't recall touching you that way last night," he said carefully, and felt an unwelcome twinge of satisfaction when her cheeks flamed.

"No. Oh, no. Last night…last night for a moment you forgot, didn't you? You forgot who I was and what I was, and you touched me like a woman."

He watched her with a frown, not at all sure now where this was coming from. "Do you want me to be sorry about that? Am I supposed to be sorry for kissing you?"

"Aren't you? Aren't you sorry? Sorry about that and about agreeing to this…this arrangement of a marriage?"

There were tears now. Big and bright and brimming and winning the battle with her pride. He didn't know what to say to her. She, however, had plenty to say.

"It's not that I expect you to…to love me. Not…not right away. But I thought…last night…I thought you at least wanted me. But you don't see me as anything but an obligation, do you? And why wouldn't you? That's all I am. That's all I've ever been."

"Ellie—"

"Don't! Do not talk to me like I'm a child. I am a woman. And for better or worse, I am your wife!" Violet eyes, wild with hurt and anger, glared him. Then, with a frustrated kitten's roar, she made a small, tight fist and popped him in the chest.

She roared again when he just stood there, unfazed

by the physical blow but stunned by the fury and passion that had prompted it.

"I am supposed to be your partner, not your charge! And I have epilepsy, not the plague. You can't catch it. If it scares you or repulses you, I'm sorry. I can't control what you feel. I can't control the disease. But that doesn't mean I can't be your wife if you would just give me the chance."

His head was swimming—at the depth of her anger—at the source of the pain that had prompted someone so gentle and kind to physically strike out. At the words she'd fired at him like bullets. One word in particular. She thought she repulsed him?

While he was still reeling, she tugged off her apron, threw it in his general direction and ran out the kitchen door.

Tossing the apron aside, he turned off the burners on the stove and stormed after her, wincing his way across the gravel on bare feet and followed her to the barn.

It was quiet as he shouldered through the door and eased inside. It was also dark. His eyes adjusted slowly until he found her there, a spot of spring in her pretty dress as she pressed her face against Bud's neck and let the tears flow.

He was leery of touching her so he stood by her side, one hand on the big gelding's withers. "Ellie...you don't repulse me. You *so* don't repulse me. I want you. With every breath I draw, I want you."

She didn't look at him. And only after a very long, doubtful silence, did she quietly ask, "Then why? Why did you...why did you do that to me last night?"

He watched her carefully before he finally spoke

and even then he felt totally out of sync with the workings of her mind. "I thought you liked it. I thought you liked it when I touched you."

"I did. I...I did," she finished softly, her voice muffled against Bud's neck. "But then...then you left me. Alone again. You gave me something... something that made me feel wonderful and powerful and...and strong. And then you took it away when you wouldn't let me give it back to you."

He closed his eyes, pressed his forehead against the hand he'd formed into a fist on Bud's broad neck as the light finally dawned. "Baby, that's not why I left. You were exhausted. It was late. I didn't want to take advantage." How could he say this without making matters worse? "I didn't want to take you further than you were prepared to go."

"So you made a decision. For my benefit." The steel was back in her voice. So was the heat.

"Yes," he said carefully.

He knew he'd been hung by his own rope even before she quietly murmured, "Like my keeper."

He drew in a deep breath, let it out and bit the bullet. "Like someone who cares about you. I see now that I was wrong to take that choice away from you.

"Ellie, please look at me." He waited for her to do just that, and when she finally did, he saw how deep his error in judgment had cut her. "I'm on shaky ground here. I'm not doing a very good job of..." he trailed off, searching for the words, but before he found them, she found some for him.

"Of taking care of me."

"Yes," he admitted again even though he knew it

might set her off. "Of taking care of you. It's not a bad thing. I *want* to take care of you."

"I thought we agreed to take care of each other."

Okay. So he'd sold her short on that one, too. "You're right. Again. We did agree to take care of each other. But I can't...hell." He dragged a hand roughly through his hair, felt the ground he'd gained shift, like sand, beneath his feet and settled himself down.

"I want to make love to you," he said candidly and saw her reaction through her soulful, searching eyes. "After last night I don't know how much longer I can hold out.

"But I don't want to hurt you," he added, trying to make her understand. "I don't ever want to put you in a position where I could hurt you."

She let out a deep breath, sectioned off a small handful of Bud's mane and started absently working it with her hands. "I get so tired of being a...consideration," she said at last as she began the intricate but automatic process of making a braid. "I just want to be seen as a person—not a person with a problem."

He'd hurt her again but he'd be damned if he'd apologize. "Would you rather I didn't care? Would you rather I didn't consider your health?"

Another long, weary sigh. "I'd rather this wasn't a part of me. But it is."

The long silence that followed underscored the fact that it was his wish too. That was the bottom line, and they both knew it as she forked her fingers through the braid she'd just completed and smoothed it back as it had been. Then she turned to him with those beautiful, troubled eyes.

"You can't fix me," she said at last. "Even though you want to."

He frowned. "Ellie, no—"

"You think I don't see what you've been doing? Every day since you've been here, you've charged around like a man possessed. Fixing this. Fixing that. But you can't fix me, Lee," she repeated, daring him to deny the truth of her conclusion.

He had to look away. It was true. That's exactly what he'd wanted to do—and she'd figured it out before he had. He'd wanted to fix what he had control over because he had no control over what the epilepsy did to her. Suddenly he was ashamed.

"You say you don't want to hurt me? Then you need to accept me. As I am. The epilepsy is part of me. It's not going away. Ever."

He drew in a weary breath, let it out, met her eyes. "Then help me understand," he said gently. "Help me know what you deal with."

"So you'll know how to take care of me," she concluded, driving her point home with a bite that didn't quite rally what she'd lost of her pride.

"Yes," he said, honestly. "But more than that. I want to know. I want to know you better. For all the reasons you just said. The epilepsy is part of you. I'm your husband. That makes it part of me.

"Help me, Ellie. Help me understand so I don't go on hurting you."

He was asking a lot of her. He knew it; so did she.

When she turned to him, it wasn't so much with acceptance as it was with defeat. He saw in her eyes, her sad, brave eyes that she'd reconciled herself to the idea that it was the only way they could start getting past this. Reconciled, that's all.

He held out his hand, determined that she would never be sorry for anything she shared with him.

After what seemed like an eternity, she reached out, took his hand.

He didn't feel the strength in her hand today, only the reluctance that trembled through her. And the fear of rejection that she'd lived with too long and that he promised himself she would never feel again. Not from him.

He led her back to the house. Sat down with her on his lap in the big wicker chair on the front porch. And he just held her that way and rocked her until, with the spring breeze humming through her wind chimes, she slowly, and with grim determination, started telling him things she'd never told another living soul.

They were late for church. He couldn't help but smile as one of Clare's favorite platitudes came to mind.

"Timing's not as important as presence. Showing up's what counts, not being early or late, but just being."

Being, however, was different from belonging. Lee had never belonged. Every time he stepped through the double, arched doorway of the Sundown Congregational Church, he expected to hear the creak and groan of the roof giving way and falling in on his head—if for no other reason than the shock of seeing him there.

As a ten-year-old boy he'd never been inside a church until Will and Clare had dragged him here, practically kicking and screaming. He still felt that odd sense of a benevolent but judgmental presence, a supreme power, whenever he sat before the altar and the music swelled out of the ancient organ and rang out over the congregation.

Hard as Clare had tried, he still considered himself more sinner than saint. Except for attending Clare's and then Will's funeral and his own wedding ceremony last week, he'd seldom found his way inside of any church in the past several years. Even so, there were some things he hadn't forgotten—like the peace that settled over him as he walked Ellie toward the Shiloh family pew.

Beside him she was quiet, just as she'd been quiet on the ride to town. He understood why. He'd been quiet, too. He had a lot to think about. And he had a big reason to hope that Doc Lundstrum could fill in some of the blanks that Ellie had left empty.

Starting today he wanted to be more to her than he had been. Because he understood now. He understood that he wasn't the only one who felt as if they had never belonged.

He wanted to be more than her protector; he wanted to be things he still couldn't be for her, not through any failing of hers but because there were some things he still wasn't capable of. Like the fairy-tale love she wanted and deserved.

But he could be her husband. He wanted to be her husband. Not because he was bound by duty, he'd realized with no small measure of surprise. But because he wanted to be someone important to her. Because she deserved to have someone who wanted to be important to her.

And he wanted to make love to her. He wanted it to be tonight.

The sun was clear and high as they walked outside

after the service and people broke off into little pockets of conversation. Lee stood by himself, a little surprised that Peg Lathrop had practically attacked Ellie and pulled her aside. The two of them were locked in conversation at the edge of the aspen grove that flanked the church on three sides. Peg's little girl, a five-year-old tomboy with blond braids and a grass stain on the knee of her Sunday school dress, was busy playing on the swing set that was part of the city park playground adjacent to the church grounds.

Lee stood on the bottom step, a hand in the pocket of his suit pants, and squinted against the sun that was only an hour away from noon.

"How's it going, young man?"

He turned to see Doc's bushy brows pinched together in question and breathed a sign of relief. Cutting a look toward Ellie and Peg and seeing that they were still deep in conversation, he steered Doc aside.

"You got a minute?" he asked Doc, but didn't wait for confirmation as he maneuvered him toward the corner of the church where they could have some privacy.

"What's on your mind, son?" Doc asked.

"We need to have that talk now."

Doc drummed his blunt-tipped fingers over his robust belly that was covered in a crisp white dress shirt and a slim paisley print tie. "Well now. It's about time. It sure is about time."

Later that afternoon Lee sat on the ridge above the valley that overlooked Shiloh. Bud shifted beneath him, the saddle leather creaking as the old gelding resettled his weight.

Below, in the house by herself, Lee knew that Ellie

was wondering. Wondering and waiting and reading a hundred different messages into his distance and his silence.

He wished that he could have saved her that anxiety. But he'd needed some time. To absorb. To digest. To acclimatize himself to the glut of information he'd received today from both Ellie and Doc.

After church he'd taken her out to dinner at the Dusk to Dawn, Sundown's one and only restaurant, bar and youth center all rolled up into one. She had protested at first. He'd overridden her feeble excuses. He'd wanted to show her a thousand reasons why he didn't put any stock in her fears.

Afterward he'd been sorry that he'd forced the experience on her. She'd been uncomfortable, self-conscience. Miserable. While he recognized some of the faces, many, he didn't. And many had stared—or tried not to.

He needed time to deal with that, too. With what those stares did to her.

So once they'd gotten home, he'd changed into his work clothes, kissed her tenderly and saddled up Bud. Then he'd headed out to check the herd. That had been nearly three hours ago. He wasn't really needed out here. Most of the mares had dropped their foals before he'd returned to Shiloh last week, but there were a few holdouts, so it was a good excuse to see how they were making out.

But she'd known. She'd known as well as he had that he needed some room to draw conclusions, make decisions, deal with what he now knew that he'd never known before.

There were so many terms. So much information.

So much of it hard to accept. Big deal. It was hard for him; she lived it. What must it be like for her?

He dismounted, ground-reined Bud and let him graze. Then he lay down on his back in the pasture grass. Crossing his arms behind his head, he stared at wispy clouds that drifted like mare's tails across acres of blue Montana sky. He used to do this a lot when he was a kid. Laze around in the sun. Think and brood. Later in the summer this pasture would be alive with colors—the brilliant yellow of wild buttercups, the burnt orange of Indian paintbrush, the soft lavender of harebells.

Lavender, like Ellie's eyes.

Ellie.

"Partial complex seizures," Doc had said. "No, no son. Surgery's not a good option for her, although we did consider it for a time. She does well on her medication."

Anticonvulsants. Phenytoin, phenobarbital. And more. Some he couldn't pronounce or remember.

"She hates them," he'd told Doc, confiding what Ellie had confessed, trying to understand why.

"I know. She remembers when she first started on them, or the times we've had to adjust. The side effects are always more noticeable when we have to mess with her meds, but then her body settles in, the chemistry becomes more balanced and the effects aren't as severe."

Dry mouth, periods of depression, sluggishness.

The epilepsy wasn't bad enough. She had to live with the treatment, too.

"The medication has done a remarkable job managing her seizures," Doc had added. "We always have to keep that in mind."

"What causes them?"

Doc had shrugged. "It's not always something we can pinpoint. With Ellie we suspect it was a birth trauma. And at this point it really doesn't matter. The results and the treatments are the same."

"What happens? What, exactly, happens to her?"

Doc had frowned as he thought to formulate a response. "There are innumerable cells in our brains, and they normally work in perfect harmony—relaying the electrical and chemical signals that allow us to tell a story or clap our hands or even to feel happy. With Ellie things work smoothly most of the time. But sometimes certain brain cells go haywire and misfire. That's when she has a seizure."

More helplessness. More questions. "What triggers them?"

Doc had shrugged again. "When she was little, it was usually a fever. Any time she cut a tooth, got the flu. Puberty was especially hard on her—all the hormonal changes. Now her seizures are mostly controlled. But sometimes, if she gets too stressed or too tired…" He'd trailed off, lifted a hand as if to say, you never know. "Sometimes it's nothing at all. It just happens. No explanation."

He remembered what she'd told him this morning. "She says she hears chimes."

"Her aura," Doc had said with a nod. "With Ellie, her warning aura comes in the form of chimes. Sometimes, if she tunes in soon enough, she can actually forestall an episode, or at least diminish the severity if she can lie down in a dark, quiet room and just wait it out."

"But not always."

"No. Unfortunately, not always."

The shadow of a bald eagle, its wingspread as wide as a small car, sailed overhead. Lee watched it soar, wished for that kind of freedom for Ellie.

"What do I do?" he'd asked Doc. "When she has a seizure. What do I do?"

"Just give her room. If you're around when it happens don't crowd her. And unless it lasts for more than two or three minutes, don't panic. Anything more, you get on the phone and you call me. She'll be in a form of suspended consciousness. You may think she's alert, but she's not. She may speak, but she doesn't know she's talking and what she says may not make sense to you. She may roll her wrist, or pick at things... Clare once told me that she usually has busy hands...like she's buttoning and unbuttoning nonexistent buttons. That sort of thing. She won't be violent. She won't be self-destructive. She may lie down or just sit. But if you crowd her, she might become frightened, distraught. So you just leave her be, make sure that if she's up and walking that you keep tabs on her so she doesn't hurt herself.

"And when it's over," Doc continued, "you help her cope. She won't remember it but she'll have a humdinger of a headache, and she'll be disoriented for a while. She'll also be as exhausted as if she'd run a marathon. And then she'll have to mourn the fact that she's lost a little bit of herself again. I think that's the hardest for her. Knowing that she was completely vulnerable, not knowing what she did, how she acted."

As the sun beat down, Lee remembered the way his breath had felt huge and thick in his chest as he'd listened to Doc. "How does she deal with it?" he'd asked aloud, without even knowing he'd said the words.

Doc had laid a hand on his arm. "Son, she deals with it like a trooper. She's one of the most adjusted individuals I have the pleasure of knowing. You've probably already figured that out for yourself, though. She could be angry. She could be bitter. She could be frightened and insecure. She's none of those things. Oh, I know she has her moments, but, for the long haul, she's solid."

Lee closed his eyes. He'd given her some of those moments with his own insecurity, his own ignorance and inability to get this out in the open. She had been so right this morning in the barn. He did want to fix things for her. He was a man of action. He felt crippled by his inability to help her, just as he was crippling her by not allowing her to be what she needed to be for him.

"Acceptance of herself, of her epilepsy are the most critical factors to help her live with it," Doc had added meaningfully. "It's also critical for you to accept it if you hope to develop the kind of relationship you'll both need to see you through the tough times."

Doc had looked at his boots, looked at the sky.

"But I reckon you've already got that part figured out, too. It's the other part of the relationship that's worrying you now."

"I don't want to hurt her," he'd said quietly.

"But you want her," Doc had concluded.

He'd pushed out a disgusted snort. "What does that make me?"

Lee hadn't seen anything funny but Doc had laughed. "Why, it makes you a red-blooded American male, son. And it makes her a lucky woman. The only thing you could do to hurt her is to refuse to let her be a wife to you.

"Look, Lee, Ellie is experiencing all the feelings a bride is supposed to feel—along with some that no bride should have to contend with. She has to deal with the reality of her epilepsy—with the moments it steals from her life, the strength it saps from her psyche, with the cost to her pride. Most of all she has to deal with the differential treatment she's afraid she's going to get from you because of it."

Doc had placed a fatherly hand on his shoulder. "She needs the physical part of your relationship as much as you do. Probably more and, given the male libido, that's saying quite a lot," he added with a chuckle.

Lee's scowl must have told Doc how little humor he'd found in the situation.

"Take her home, son. Love her. Give her babies."

"Babies?" He'd looked at Doc as if he'd sprouted horns.

"You don't want babies?"

He'd cupped his nape, rolled his shoulders. "Could that be good for her?"

"There's a risk, sure, but with proper monitoring and special care, she can have babies."

Lee hadn't heard anything beyond the word *risk*. There would be no babies. He would never put her at risk and was relieved to know that one of the medications she was taking to control hormonal imbalances that could worsen her symptoms was, in essence, also a form of birth control.

So that risk, at least, was factored out—but wasn't he putting her at risk right now? As he stalled for time out here on the mountain and left her alone to wonder and worry about the conclusions he had drawn, the decisions he had made—wasn't he putting her at risk with his distance?

He sat up, propped a forearm over an upraised knee and looked toward home. Where his wife waited. For him. To make her a woman.

Not much rattled him. This did. He didn't want to let her down, was determined that he wouldn't.

He rose to his feet, walked over to Bud, snagged the reins and swung into the saddle.

The setting sun followed him home.

Home to the house where, somehow, without his being aware of it happening, everything that mattered waited along with the light that burned in the bedroom window.

Eight

Ellie sat in front of her vanity mirror. The low, wide bench was upholstered in an antique satin tapestry of ivory and pink. The triple-fold antique mirror was large, its beveled glass encased in aged, lustrous oak. She could see herself from three angles; each one revealed her uncertainty about whether she'd done the right thing today.

Maybe Lee really hadn't wanted to hear some of the things she'd told him this morning. Maybe he hadn't liked what Doc had told him, either. She'd seen their heads together after church. While Peg had pumped her for information and she'd done her best to assure her that everything was wonderful and that Peg's plan had worked, she'd worried that they had actually drifted further apart instead of closer together.

Hadn't he left her alone all afternoon? Hadn't he

ridden out with excuses about checking on the herd and then stayed away until almost sundown?

She dropped her silver-filigree brush to her lap, ran her fingers across the bristles. She didn't want to spend another night alone in her bed.

Why had she told him so much? Why had she told him that one story in particular? She stared, without seeing, at the mirror. A soft light burned by the bed, illuminating her reflection. She'd had her bath, pulled on her old pink chenille robe and sat down to brush her hair.

She wouldn't wear her honeymoon gown tonight. She figured there would be no need. If Lee hadn't wanted her before, he couldn't want her, now that he knew so many more things about her.

Some places were harder to go to than others. The day that she'd told him about this morning had been one of them. She'd never talked about it before. Not even with her mother. She'd been fifteen and she'd been scared. Why, oh, why had she told Lee?

Because he'd felt so solid and strong as she'd sat on his lap that the story had just tumbled out.

"I rode Bud up to the north pasture one day," she'd begun, hearing her voice as if it belonged to someone else, seeing herself in the sunshine riding Bud bareback, his hide warm and solid and wide between her legs. "I was fifteen. I'd taken Daddy lunch. On the way back..." She'd stopped, swallowed, concentrated on remembering the warmth of the sun, the bear grass and fireweed dancing in the breeze, the hawk she'd spotted riding the wind currents.

"On the way back, I cut over to Mile High Pass so I could ride part of the way on the road. I'd seen a spring fawn at Miller's Creek the week before, and

I thought maybe I'd get lucky and it would be there again.''

She hadn't been able to look at him as she'd talked, and even now, all these hours later, she remembered staring at her hands that were gripped so tightly together her knuckles had turned white.

"This old truck came barreling down the road, kicking up gravel, stirring up a dust trail. It was almost on Bud and me before they saw us and slammed on the brakes. Bud bolted and dumped me in the ditch.''

Lee's big hands had stroked her back.

"I wasn't hurt. Humiliated, but not hurt. I took off walking after him but he was hell-bent on home. I was still dusting myself off when I heard them behind me.''

She stopped. Swallowed. "I'd...I'd seen them before. Once at the feed store. Once at the Stop and Shop. They were brothers—new in Sundown—and I'd heard Momma and Dad say that they were bad news.''

Just like this morning when she'd told her story to Lee, her vision got blurry, and she felt the hot sting of tears, tasted the salt of them in the corner of her mouth.

"I...I could smell their breath when they...when they started walking beside me. They'd been drinking.''

She'd felt Lee's hard body tense beneath her. Heard him say her name.

"I was so scared. They were...they were so mean. They laughed and made fun of me. 'You're Ellie, right? Ellie Shiloh? We heard about you. You throw fits, don't ya? Crazy as loon, right? But hey—you're kinda cute so what do you say Ellie? What you got under that shirt there? How about goin' crazy with us?'"

Even now she remembered both the humiliation of that day and the contrast of Lee's arms wrapped around her this morning. For a moment all the hurt, all the shame those boys had made her feel, had eased back into the past where it belonged. Where it couldn't touch her.

"They hurt you," he'd said, his voice hard and cold and edged with something that traced a trail of fear down her spine and made her shiver.

"No. They didn't touch me. They just humiliated me. And scared me. I got so scared that I...I had a seizure. When I came...came back to myself, they were gone. They'd just left me there."

She'd swallowed, stared at her hands. "They didn't know if I would be all right or if I needed help. They just left me. Like—"

She hadn't said it. But she'd felt what she'd left unsaid many times over the years. Like she was nothing—or worse than nothing. Like she was something revolting.

She'd tried for a smile. "Guess I scared them more than they scared me, huh?"

Lee had been quiet for a long time when she'd finally looked up and met his eyes. She'd seen rage, compassion and something she hadn't understood then but thought she understood now.

He wasn't here. That was all the understanding she needed.

She heard a sound behind her—the creak of a floor-board. Her heart jumped, with something that was more surprise than hope.

She didn't turn around. For the longest time she didn't even look up. She stared at her hands, at her fingers wrapped around the silver brush handle and wished she knew what to do, what to say to the man who stood in the doorway to her bedroom.

Finally she gathered her courage, lifted her head and met his reflection in her vanity mirror.

And her heart skipped several beats.

He'd showered—evidently in the basement, because she'd never heard him in the upstairs bathroom. Like the night they'd come home from the Fergusons, his hair was still wet. She should be used to seeing him this way. Her heart shouldn't flutter so. But it did as he stood there in his bare feet and blue jeans, his shirt hanging open, the tails falling loose at his hips.

Between the open placket of his shirt, she could see the softly curling hair that covered his chest and arrowed down his hard abdomen to disappear beneath jeans that were zipped but not snapped. Her gaze was riveted there, at that spot where denim met flesh, and the slight rise and fall of that beautifully taut skin was the only indication that he was a living, breathing man, not a figment of her imagination.

She swallowed and finally raised her gaze to his. And her heart stopped. In the diluted bedroom light, in the reflection of her mirror, she saw the deep-blue of his irises, the dark intensity of his bold stare.

He watches you.

In her mind she heard Peg's words, remembered how he had looked at her the night of the shivaree.

He was watching her now...the way he had watched her last night on the porch, just before he'd kissed her.

And then she heard Lee's words, like a song that floated on the cusp of her memory.

Not want you? I have wanted you for what seems like forever.

Her reservations forgotten, her insecurities locked back in that place from which they had escaped, she held his gaze.

And smiled.

Her smile was heartbreaking, head-spinning. It was full of wonder, full of trust. Full of a love Lee was sure he didn't deserve but was determined to never betray. She had more than enough reason to feel angry and confused and insecure. And yet she sat there, with her strong, brave heart. Waiting for him. Eager for him. Smiling for him.

He wanted her so much in that moment, he thought he would explode with it. She wouldn't want to hear it, but now, more than ever, he needed to take care with her. Not just because of what he'd learned about her disease—but because of how huge his need had grown. And because she deserved the best he could give her.

And, yeah, there was more to it than that. He'd not only learned things about her today, he'd learned a few things about himself. It was still a tough pill to swallow, but if he were being utterly, brutally honest, he had to admit that it hadn't been Ellie as much as himself that he'd really been trying to protect all this time. What he felt for her...what she did to him.

It wasn't just this tightening in his chest when he looked at her, the constant craving of his physical need when he touched her. The feelings she was dragging out of him he hadn't even known were there, they'd been buried so deep, protected so well by years of building shields.

It scared the hell out of him to think about letting the barriers down. But his fears were nothing compared to the fears she had to overcome on a daily basis.

He flexed his fingers, realized his palms were sweating. And then she said his name, in welcome, in anticipation, in the wonderful way she had of making him feel like the one man, the only man, the most important man on earth.

And he quit thinking. He just felt.

Sundown had come and gone. The small bedside lamp glowed softly, casting the room and her face in gentle shadows. It made him want to see her by candlelight. It made him want to make love to her under the stars.

Her hair was loose. It spilled down her back and drifted across her shoulders like a cloud, trailed like a spool of vibrant, curling ribbons over her breasts.

He went to her. Pressed a knee onto the bench beside her hip and felt, more than heard, her sigh as she leaned back against him. Her eyes were warm and searching as she met his in the mirror; her hair was cool against his skin as it grazed his belly.

Without a word he gathered the curling mass in his hand. Heavy, like satin. Thick, like sable. He inhaled the honeyed scent of it and leaned toward her. Her breath trembled out on a sweet little catch, her fingers suddenly limp on the handle of her delicate silver brush as he eased it from her hand.

"You are so beautiful." He met her gaze in the mirror. Her violet eyes, misty with anticipation, followed the motions of his hands as he gathered her hair, draped it over her left shoulder, then began brushing with slow, long strokes.

"That…feels…wonderful," she whispered as she relaxed against him, the back of her head pressing against his bare abdomen, her shoulders nestled between his hip points. His erection pulsed, huge and hot between her shoulder blades. "*You* feel wonderful," she added, turning her head slowly from side to side, caressing him with her eyes and that slight, subtle pressure.

"Tell me what you want, Ellie," he managed, aching with need, determined to please her, then please her some more.

"I wish…I wish I'd worn my white gown," she said shyly.

With the brush still gripped in his hand, he rested his hands on her shoulders. "But you look so pretty in pink." He smiled when she blushed. "Even prettier out of it."

Very slowly he stroked the cool silver back of the brush along the curve of her jaw. She shivered, and with her eyes closed in sensory pleasure, reached back and gripped his thighs with her small hands.

"Open your eyes, Ellie," he commanded on a gruff whisper. "Look. Look how pretty you are."

With slow, pleasured languor, she obeyed. He watched her eyes fill with wonder and fascination. The picture she made—the picture they made together—equally fascinated him.

She was so pale and delicate; he was dark, muscled and rough around the edges. He was stunned by the contrast, yet it helped him get a firmer grip on the importance of making this good for her.

Torn between watching her face and the progress

of his hand, he lowered the brush and with deliberate, downward motions, caressed her slender throat with the same sensual motion. Cool silver touched warm, flushed skin and he felt another delicate little shiver eddy through her body.

He edged the brush under the robe's lapel, pushed it aside. Her breasts rose and fell sharply, straining against the fabric as he leaned forward, found the loosely knotted belt at her waist and, with a gentle tug, pulled it free. Her robe fell open to reveal a deep vee of pale, creamy flesh, wide at her shoulders, narrowing to a slender opening just below her navel.

"So pretty," he whispered, and, setting the brush aside, splayed his fingers wide at her throat, then over her collarbone and slowly pushed the pink chenille down her arms, baring her breasts to the night.

A slow shudder passed through his body as he watched her reflection in the mirror. Watched her eyes cloud over with a sensual haze, watched his hands, work roughened and as big as bear paws glide over her delicate flesh where they rested just above the gentle round at the top of her breasts.

He was mesmerized by the contrasts, by her heat, by the velvet softness of her nipples that tightened into stiff little peaks as he lowered his hands, covered her, then filled his palms with the soft, resilient weight of her.

She liked it—she liked him touching her this way, and he loved experiencing her reaction when he ground his palms against her, then shaped her with his fingers, lifted and flicked the tips of his thumbs over those velvety hard little beads.

When he lightly pinched, then rolled, her erect nipples between his thumb and forefinger, she clutched wildly at his thighs, then, with an urgency that thickened his pulse, raised her arms above her head, reaching for him, arching her sweet breasts deeper into his hands.

He lost it then. Caressing her breast with one hand, he dragged the other hand up her chest, bracketed her jaw in his hand and tipped her head back for a deep, searing kiss.

Touching her wasn't enough. Tasting her wasn't enough. He wanted her tongue. And he took it, then showed her with an intimate ebb and flow, a calculated stroke and withdrawal that he wanted more than his tongue inside her, more than his mouth invading her sweet, giving body.

He wanted in a way he'd never wanted anything in his life. He wanted to own her. He wanted to be owned by her. Heart. Body. Soul. He poured everything that he was into that kiss, told her with the hands that held her, the body that burned for her that she was the one, the only one he wanted or needed or desired.

Ellie's head was spinning. Her blood was flying through her veins, throbbing at her pulse points and lower, woman low. She ached there. She burned. She yearned with all that was in her to know what a wife should know about the physical love that only her husband could show her.

"Make love to me," she begged against his mouth, his busy, busy mouth that was devouring hers, worshiping hers, telling her with his kisses that tonight would not be like the others. Tonight he wasn't leaving her.

Strong arms banded around her and lifted her as if

she weighed no more than a feather. He carried her across the room to the bed, where he laid her down.

He stood above her, like a dark angel, like a man who saw only his woman, and roughly shrugged his shirt from his shoulders and stripped it down his arms. She hiked herself up on her elbows, not wanting to miss anything, not one move, not one single event as he reached for his zipper and drew it down.

He stopped abruptly, his thumbs hooked beneath the denim at his waistband, where his skin was pale and that arrow of silky, dark hair narrowed and disappeared out of sight.

"Do you have any idea..." His voice sounded raspy and rough, and he swallowed as his blue gaze strafed her body then returned to her face. "Do you have any idea how incredible you look?"

She blinked slowly, then looked down at herself. She should probably be embarrassed. The warm flush she felt spreading in tiny, tingling fingers beneath her skin told her she was, at least a little.

But the look in his eyes, oh, the look in his eyes. He made her feel achy and wanton and proud. She was completely naked. She was sprawled shamelessly on the bed. Her elbows dug into the mattress, which made her back arch and thrust her breasts forward. His gaze was fixed there, as if he couldn't get enough of looking and yet what he really wanted to do was touch.

Just like she wanted him to touch her. With his hands. With his mouth.

"Please," she whispered, and lay back down on the bed, lifting her arms in reckless abandon to lie, palms up, on the pillow by her head.

He peeled his jeans and briefs down his hips and

shoved them down his legs—and she couldn't stop staring.

He…he wasn't exactly like the pictures in the book that even now lay tucked between her mattress and springs at the edge of the bed. He was—he was more. He was better.

He was bigger. Much, much bigger. And for a moment, to her mortification, she felt the stinging pinch of anxiety.

What if…what if—

"Ellie."

Her gaze flashed from that part of him that was so fascinating and so male to his face as he eased a hip on the corner of the bed. He was smiling as he reached out, brushed an errant curl away from the corner of her mouth.

"Tell me what you're thinking," he demanded softly.

She swallowed, then groaned when his fingertips drifted across the round of her breast, then returned to cup her, mold her in his palm.

"That…that you're beautiful," she managed, and covered his hand with hers, riding the motion of his hand, forgetting that she'd been concerned and instead drifted on sensation.

"And?" he continued as he lowered his mouth where his hand had been.

"And, umm. Oh…" She squirmed, needing to be closer, begging him without words to keep on doing those wonderful things he was doing.

"And what, baby?"

"And…and that you're very, very big." The words spilled out on a restless sigh, and then, realizing what she'd said, she opened her eyes to see what he made of that.

He chuckled softly and lay down beside her. "We'll fit just fine," he told her, drawing her snugly against his side. "I'll make sure of it."

"You will?" She threaded her fingers through his hair as he moved from one breast to the other to sip and savor, lick and softly nip. "H-how?"

"By doing what I'm doing. Am I making you want me, Ellie?"

"Yes. Oh, yes," she exclaimed without inhibition.

"Am I making you wet?"

"Yes. I'm…sorry."

He lifted his head. "Sorry? Ellie, it's beautiful. The way you feel." His hand trailed down her abdomen, found her curls, covered her with his palm, then with the drift of a finger, delved into warm, slick flesh. "Wet," he murmured, as he brushed his open mouth over hers, catching the sigh that escaped her parted lips. "You are wonderful. And wet. Just for me."

"I…I get that way sometimes," she confessed, as her hips moved involuntarily with the slow, wondrous motion of his finger. Inside her. Stroking her. Moving her toward something she craved. Something she couldn't describe but didn't know how she'd ever lived without. "Sometimes," she tried again breathlessly, "sometimes, all I have to do is think about you. About, oh—" she shivered when he touched her deep "—about your mouth."

The mouth in question crushed down on hers. A deep growl sounded low in his throat as he moved over her, supporting his weight on his elbows, edging a powerful knee between her thighs.

She drowned in the kiss, then floated in the wonder

of it and all the feelings he'd coaxed to life with just the gentle probe of his finger, the delicious pressure and skillful strokes.

She gazed up at him, her eyes dreamy in anticipation of more.

"What?" he asked, responding to the yearning in her eyes. "What do you want? Tell me, Ellie. It's yours."

"I want your hand back," she said a little desperately. "Where it was."

"Do you now?" he murmured with a smile in his voice and dropped the most tender kisses on her cheek, then on her brow before returning to her mouth. "What else do you want?"

She swallowed, closed her eyes, hardly believing what was coming out of her mouth. "Your...your finger. Why did you take it away?"

For a moment he just stared at her, then his beautiful mouth curved up into a smile so tender, so indulgent, she forgot about being embarrassed.

"You liked that?"

She nodded and felt her cheeks flame.

"You're going to like this even better," he promised and with exquisite care, reached down between their bodies and guided that part of him—that very big part of him—to the spot where his finger had been.

She closed her eyes as he rested there, just rested with a steady, heavy pressure.

"Ellie?"

"Hmm," she sighed dreamily and because she couldn't not, lifted her hips, just a little, increasing the contact, enhancing the sensation as her body stretched, accommodated and allowed him penetration.

She caught her breath. He groaned. She opened her eyes. His were pinched tightly shut. The veins on his neck were bulging, his lips compressed like he was in pain.

"What's wrong? What's wrong?" she whispered urgently.

The sound he made fell somewhere between a groan and a laugh. "Nothing. Lord. Not one thing." He opened his eyes then. They were dark and deep and full of passion and concern.

"Are you okay? Did I hurt you?" He ran his thumb in a gentle caress along the line of her brow.

She thought about it, about the sharp, biting sting that had already settled into a distant, pulsing ache that only made her wonder and want more. She shook her head, her gaze locked on his and pressed her small hands against his hips. "More. Please."

He closed his eyes, swallowed hard. "How did I ever get so lucky to have you? In my life. In my bed."

Lucky? He was lucky? To have her? To have *her?* A rush of love so intense, so profound filled her chest—as her husband filled her body. Little by little. Inch by precious inch.

She bit her lower lip between her teeth, felt tears sting her eyes.

"I'm sorry."

"No. No. Don't...don't go," she begged, when he started to withdraw. She clutched his hips in her hands, holding him close, keeping him near. "It's...it's just so...good. Stay. Please, please stay with me."

Above her, her husband, her husband who filled her body in the most intimate, most cherished of ways, smiled. "I can make it better."

An incredulous laugh escaped her. "Better?"

"Trust me."

"I do. Oh, I do."

A look crossed his face then—a look so tender, so deeply touching—and warmed her in places that had nothing and everything to do with this physical joining that bound them together as husband and wife. She wanted to tell him…how he made her feel…how much she loved him. But he started moving inside her then. A slow, lazy withdrawal that stopped her heart—a long, deep penetration that sent it racing and stole all coherent thought.

Over and over he entered and withdrew. And he was right. It *was* better. It was…it was… "Lee…"

"I know, baby. Let it happen."

Trust. It was all about trust. She let herself fly free, let herself tumble, head over heels out of control into the fall.

Heat. Flight. Heaven. He took her there. He took her beyond, and for the first time in her life she willingly and without reservation gave in to a power that stole those most precious pieces of what made her whole. Her sense of time, her sense of place, her sense of self. She gave them over to his keeping—completely consumed, utterly lost in the shelter of her husband's loving arms.

Lee had forgotten about Montana mornings like this—where the cool was so pure you could breathe it. Where the sun was so crystalline and bright it cut through the chill as it edged over the mountain ridge and flooded the valley with light. In Texas it would already be so hot this time of day you could feel the weight of it pressing down from above even as it pushed back up from the baked earth until you felt wedged in the middle of an oven.

He stood on the front porch, drank from the mug of coffee he'd brought outside with him. And thought of his wife. All silky and warm and snuggled deeply in the covers of her bed where he'd left her sleeping. Of *their* bed, he amended with a smile and set the coffee aside. He headed for the barn, hurried through the chores, then climbed the stairs to join her there again.

He was quiet as he entered the bedroom, silently shucked his clothes and slid back beneath the covers beside the sweetest heat, the most delicate flesh.

She warmed him like a fire. But she needed to sleep. So he tried. He really tried to lie there, to let her be, to content himself with her softness snuggled against him. To let it be enough.

But it wasn't enough, and he was beginning to wonder when he would ever get enough of her. It played hell on a man's ego to realize that one tiny little woman could turn him inside out like this, and all she had to do to accomplish it was sleep.

She lay there with her hair spilling across her pillow and sunshine slanting into the room. He loved the look of her by daylight. He loved the tiny sprinkling of freckles that dusted the bridge of her nose and the soft slope of her shoulders like angel fire. He loved the snuffling little sleep sounds she made when she curled into him and pressed her face into the hollow of his throat.

He loved her.

It hit him like a velvet punch.

He loved her.

He loved.

He—Lee Savage—loved.

He waited for the denial. For the profound and pathetic panic that always edged in whenever he even skirted the perimeters of a territory he'd always considered uncharted, overromanticized and, for him, unattainable.

He tried it again. He loved her. He waited again for the thundering heartbeat, for the inconsolable urge to run. For the anger that reminded him he wasn't capable, couldn't possibly be entitled to anything this good.

Nothing.

Just peace.

Just...love. Sweet, healing love.

Man, oh, man, who'd have thought it. From the beginning he'd planned on a physical relationship. He'd counted on affection. He hadn't anticipated this emotional commitment she'd dragged out of him with her undeniable trust. Her true and honest giving.

It rocked him. And in an unexpected way it also anchored him, as he'd never felt anchored. He'd thought he could physically love her without giving too much of himself away. Hell, it had worked for him for thirty-three years. But with Ellie he'd not only dropped all of his shields, he'd walked over them, left them in the dust.

Will and Clare, for all they had given him, for all he had cared for them, they'd never gotten past his defenses. They'd never gotten this deep. Not soul deep the way she had.

He loved this woman. And he couldn't help himself

any longer. He folded back the covers, hiked himself up on an elbow and simply watched her sleep. His wife.

Her breasts were so pale, her areolas so deliciously pink and delicately pebbled around the tip of her nipples. Even as she slept, they knotted into tight little beads.

He glanced up, saw that her eyes were open, watchful.

"Good morning, Mrs. Savage." His hand moved automatically to her breast, drawn, as his gaze was drawn to her eyes.

She stretched and pressed into his hand. "Good morning, Mr. Savage."

They shared a smile then, one full of longing and memories and discoveries they'd made in this bed. He'd made love to her again after that first time. After he'd gently bathed the signs of her virginity from her thighs, he'd taken her again before he'd let her sleep. And now he wanted to do it all over again.

"I trust you slept well." He watched her face, loving the glazed look in her eyes as he played with her breast and she responded with the sweetest sigh, the most seductive little shiver.

"What time is it?"

He lowered his mouth to where his hand had been. "Close to ten."

She scrambled to sit up. "My chores—"

"Done," he informed her, and pushed her down to her back again.

"Oh. Well...but you must be hungry."

"Oh, I am. I was thinking about breakfast in bed."

She may be an innocent, but she was quick, and she was beautiful when she was coy.

"Breakfast," she said, luxuriating again in the touch of his mouth to her breast. "In bed?"

"Oh, yes, ma'am. And you don't even have to do anything."

"Nothing?"

"Just lie there," he murmured, moving over her, then moving down, nibbling, caressing, tasting as he went. The slender curve of her jaw, the delicate slope of her shoulder. The delicious tip of her breast that he couldn't seem to get enough of.

"Lee…"

"Shush. Let me. Just let me." He looked up her body, held her startled, excited gaze as his mouth cruised along her skin, to the hollow of her navel, then nipped lightly at her hip point.

He watched the fire kindle, then burst to flame as he tunneled his hands under her bottom and tilted her to his mouth.

"Let me, Ellie. Let me love you like this." He brushed his lips across her curls, feeling her tense and shiver and yearn.

He told her how beautiful she was, how perfect, as he pressed a kiss there…there where her heat was the sweetest. There where she was most sensitive, most vulnerable. There where he knew he could please her most. He wanted to take her over in a way she would never forget, in a way that would claim her absolute trust, in a way that would shatter her with pleasure.

Only he was the one who fell apart. It was a beautiful thing. The way she tasted. The way she moved. The way she moaned and cried his name when she splintered into a million fragmented pieces.

But if she was shattered by the experience, he was obliterated, bound, tied forever to the wonder of her trust, the openness of her responses. She was still coming down when he moved slowly up her body and held her while she wept softly in his arms.

And he knew. For the first time he truly understood what he was holding. In his arms he held the power to make him more than he was, more than he'd ever been. And it humbled him.

She turned in his arms then, and with her gaze intent on his, rose to her knees, took him in her hands. And destroyed him.

He bucked involuntarily against the acute, intense pleasure as she lowered her head. If he hadn't given over his heart to her before, he would have handed it to her on a platter in this moment.

"Ellie…" He dragged a hand over her tangled hair. "You don't have to."

"Oh, but I do. I have to. I want to. I need to," she whispered softly, and touched him with the tip of her tongue. "Let me. Let me…"

And he was lost.

Nine

Ellie breezed around the kitchen, hurrying to finish the dinner she'd prepared and tuck it into the oven. She wanted everything done before Lee came in from the south pasture range. She planned to feed him well. Later.

That done, the only thing on her mind was finding the bottle of wine she had ordered from the Stop and Shop for their wedding night and never had the chance to share with Lee—with her husband.

She felt the blush as it warmed her breasts, then rose to color her face before it disappeared into her hairline.

He couldn't keep his hands off her. He'd told her so. She laughed, joyful and disbelieving, and caught a glimpse of her face in the mirror that hung beside the wall phone. Hugging herself, she twirled around

in a circle, remembering the way he'd looked and
everything he'd said when he'd left her.

"I have to go do something," he'd said right after
lunch as he'd dragged her back into his arms by the
kitchen door and kissed her until she thought she'd
melt from the pleasure and the pressure of his hot
strong body pressed against hers.

"I have to…do…something. Just for a little while.
Just long enough to check the black mare—and because I won't be able to leave you alone if I stay
here."

"I'm not asking you to leave me alone," she'd
assured him, then smiled when he'd pressed his forehead to hers and groaned.

"All the more reason to go." Another quick, tender
kiss. "If you don't have the sense to shove me away,
then I'm going to have to be the one to make the
rules."

"I could go with you," she'd suggested brightly.

"No," he'd said on a deep chuckle. "You could
not! Leave it be, woman. Get some rest, because I
promise you, you're going to need it for what I have
in mind for later tonight."

Well, she thought saucily, I've got a little something in mind for tonight, too.

She blushed again thinking about it. Then she took
another long look in the mirror. She liked what she
saw. She saw a woman, not a girl. She saw a wife,
not an obligation.

And when Lee walked into the house an hour later
and found her waiting for him, naked in the middle
of their bed, the room flickering with the light of a
dozen candles and a chilled bottle of wine sitting on
the side table, she knew that he saw her that way, too.

"Ellie."

That's all he said. That's all he had to say. She opened her arms, opened her body and welcomed him home.

He lay panting and spent, spread eagled on his back in the middle of a wild tangle of sheets. Ellie sat beside him, her hands folded prayer-like under her chin, a grin as wide as the sky lighting her face.

"How did you…where did you… Good night, Ellie. How did you know how to *do* that?"

She laughed. "You didn't like it?"

He groaned. Then he laughed, too, huge and happy and utterly wasted. "I'm not sure. Maybe we ought to try it again."

She hit him with a pillow, then squealed when he reached for her. They were both laughing when he dragged her beneath him. "Talk. I mean it. Where did you learn about that?"

She groped for the side of the bed, tugged the book out from beneath the mattress and shoved it under his nose. "Page thirty-four."

With a frowning glance he set her carefully aside. When he opened the book, he blinked long and wide at the page in question, checked out the cover, looked at her smug little smile, then back at the page again.

"*Where* did you get this book?" he asked with an amazed laugh.

She tucked her feet beneath her bare bottom and brushed her hair out of her eyes. "I sent for it."

When he just stared at her, she shrugged. "Momma belonged to a book club. She used to get books on cooking and quilting and gardening…and things. They just kept sending ads. When…when I realized we were going to get married, well, I figured...I wanted to know how to make you happy. This book caught my eye.''

He laughed again, delighted, then with a wicked grin, handed it back to her. ''So...'' He reached out, toyed with a shining ribbon of hair that curled over her left breast, ''are there any other pages in there that you found noteworthy?''

''Actually...'' Looking thoughtful, she thumbed through the pages, opened the book wide, studied a picture, tilted it sideways, studied it some more, then showed it to him. ''I was kind of thinking that this looked interesting.''

He didn't even look at the book. He just looked at this woman, this amazing, inventive, brave and sensual woman he had the good fortune to call his wife. ''I so love a resourceful woman,'' he murmured as he pulled her to him. Then he tossed the book over his shoulder and showed her a little resourcefulness of his own.

He wanted to take her somewhere. It hit him while he was out checking fences about nine o'clock one morning a couple of weeks later. She needed a honeymoon. In her entire life she'd rarely been farther than Bozeman, and she needed to go someplace special. Someplace she would love and absorb and remember. As Lee rode down the lane toward the house, he wondered why he hadn't thought of it sooner.

Because he'd been so enamored with his wife, that's why. For the past two weeks he'd been completely consumed by her vast and delightful intelligence, her charming lack of guile, her extreme enthusiasm. She was bright and funny and had a wicked spark of mischief that made him laugh and reminded him that she wasn't the only one who had been missing a vital piece of her life. He'd been missing something, too—and he wasn't altogether convinced that he deserved to wake up each morning and feel such a rich, rare and indefinable warmth fill his chest when she snuggled her warm little body up next to his in bed.

It felt so good, and sometimes he couldn't help but wonder what he'd done to deserve it. In the next thought he would try very hard not to be angry with Will and Clare. They had done what they'd thought was the best thing for her, but it was clear to him now that in the process of sheltering her from a world that they wouldn't allow to corrupt or scar her, they hadn't cultivated and encouraged her boundless imagination.

She could have been so many things. He smiled, thinking about how she was making up for lost time now.

One midnight he'd awakened alone and gone looking for her. He'd found her outside. She was wearing her white gown, dancing barefoot in the starlit meadow, her fiery mop of long, tangled curls flying about her cherub face like angel hair in the moonlight. When she'd realized she'd been discovered, she'd laughed, held out her arms and damned if she hadn't had him dancing with her…and making love under the stars.

She'd coaxed him into that old claw foot tub with her more than once, too, where she'd fed him chocolate and strawberries and pressed butterfly kisses to his face with the soft flutter of her lashes.

She took him to so many places he'd never thought

he'd had in him to go. He'd discovered emotions; he'd discovered needs. He'd discovered the capacity to give in ways that stunned him; he'd discovered the ability to take and hold and trust the love she offered—and that had been the biggest surprise of all.

So, yeah, he wanted to take her somewhere, to show her how happy she made him. Because she did make him happy.

It was almost too much to digest, sometimes. He'd never figured he was entitled to this much goodness. In fact, he'd conditioned himself all of his life to live without it.

Even now, past experience raised its ugly head on a regular basis with a pat, conditioned reminder. *Something that seems too good to be true probably is. And who ever said you were entitled?*

No one. No one had ever said he was entitled to anything. And what he'd found with Ellie *did* seem too good to be true. More and more often he had to fight to outdistance the creeping sensation that not only was it too good to last, it was too rich to count on.

No sooner would he start brooding, though, and he'd see her. Like now. As he loped down the lane on Bud, he spotted her in her garden, fiery bright hair and busy hands—and a negative thought didn't have a snowball's chance in hell of denting his optimism.

She was sitting with her back to him in the middle of the freshly turned earth that he'd tilled for her just yesterday. Getting ready to plant those zinnias she'd been so anxious to get into the ground, he thought with a grin as he reined in and looped the reins over a fence post.

She was so deep in concentration that she didn't

hear him walk up behind her. With a smile of anticipation, he dropped to one knee, wrapped his arms around her and pressed a kiss to her hair.

She jumped as if he'd shot her, then tore at his arms as if he'd bound her in barbwire. Her eyes were wild, her hair flying around her face as she frantically scrambled away from him on all fours.

"No-no-no-no-no-no." A desperate, ragged whisper, a disjointed, murmured chant.

He backed off immediately, a warning shot firing through his head as she knelt there, agitated, combative, shaking her head from side to side. "No-no-no-no-no."

Seizure?

His heart rate doubled. "Ellie?"

"Sorry-sorry-sorry. I'm sorry. I'm sorry. Sorry."

He glanced quickly around, saw what he hadn't noticed before—her bucket of seed packets was scattered all over the ground like shards of colored glass. The garden hose was running, cutting a snaking river through her carefully cultivated plot.

Panicked, and afraid for her, he went to her.

She crab-walked farther away. "No-no-no-no."

He stopped abruptly as Doc's words came back to him.

Keep your distance. Don't try to restrain her. Just give her room.

He clenched his fists to his sides. It hurt. Dammit, it hurt to see her like this. Her eyes were glassy and vacant, her movements unnatural yet oddly choreographed as she sat there, hands in motion, moving her head slowly from side to side, seeing but not seeing him, speaking but not speaking to him.

"No-no-no-no-no. I'm sorry. I'm sorry. I'm sorry…"

"Ellie. Sweetheart. Can you hear me?"

"No-no-no-no-no. Don't-don't-don't-don't. Sorry-sorry. I'm s-s-sorry."

He'd never been so scared in his life. He'd never felt so helpless. But he made himself stand. Made himself stay right where he was, which was too far away.

His heart hammered as if he'd been running uphill, as a stiff breeze cooled the sweat that beaded on his brow, at the small of his back. And all he could do was stand there. Watching, worrying, agonizing over what was happening to her and pained at his utter and absolute uselessness.

He checked his watch, was debating a call to Doc when she drew in a deep breath and became utterly, disconcertingly still.

For another moment he did nothing, said nothing. And then he couldn't stand it any longer.

"Ellie?"

She sat back on her hip, lifted her hands to her face. For a long moment she just sat there and then slowly she raised her head. Her face was smudged with the dirt from her garden. Her fingers were caked with it. She looked lost. And confused. And a deep breath away from falling apart. "Lee?"

He wasn't conscious of moving, but in the next moment he was on his knees in the dirt beside her, touching a hand to her hair, soothing her with quiet words. "I'm here. I'm right here."

She swallowed several times, slowly licked her lips. "I…I…"

"Shh, baby, it's okay. I've got you. I've got you.

Let's go to the house, okay? Let's get out of the sun and get you to bed."

A tear tracked slowly down her face, cut a pale thin trail through her dust-smeared cheek.

"Lee..." With trembling hands she reached for him. His heart broke for the helplessness and hopelessness in her voice.

"I know, princess. I know."

He picked her up, cradled her in his arms and carried her to the house and up the stairs. He slowly undressed her and put her to bed. After he'd gotten a cold cloth for her head, he convinced her to take the medication that would lessen the headache that he knew would follow.

Then he pulled the curtains to darken the room, washed her face and hands, and then he just held her. He simply held her so she would know he wasn't about to let her fall apart.

Her tears were silent and hot as they fell against his throat. Her breath was irregular and ragged.

Not one word of complaint. Not one word of self-pity. Just a silence that was as heartbreaking as her tears.

Finally she slept.

He left her long enough to take care of Bud.

And then he returned, sat in the corner in the rocker and watched over her.

He thought about all the things that made her Ellie: her wonderful smiles, her buoyant enthusiasm, the little quotes she'd framed and hung here and there around the house. One in particular, by Ralph Waldo Emerson, struck a very deep cord.

"He has not learned the first lesson of life who does not every day surmount a fear."

He'd thought he'd known fear until he'd found her there. In the dirt. Lost. Alone.

He'd thought he'd known fear.

He'd been wrong.

But she knew. She surmounted fear every day of her life.

Just last night she'd confessed one of her deepest, darkest ones.

"It's the uncertainty," she'd said, snuggled in his arms after they'd made love. "It's knowing that I'll lose time that I'll never get back. I hate giving in to it. And even though, intellectually, I know I can't fight it, it still feels like a failure on my part some how."

"Ellie—"

"I know, I know. It's just hard to see past it."

She'd been quiet for a long time as she lay against his side, threading her small fingers through his chest hair.

When she spoke again, her voice had been childlike and hesitant. "I used to try to not be aware of things. Like my heartbeat. Or my breathing. Or even blinking. I was afraid that if I was too aware, I might see or feel whatever it is that's inside of me—and it would think I was inviting it. Asking it to come out.

"So I would do anything to keep from being aware. I'd sing, or talk or laugh—anything."

He hadn't known what to say. So he'd held her. And then she'd smiled up at him. "I used to be afraid. Not anymore. You gave that back to me. My self-awareness. Now I don't want to miss anything. I want to know what my body says—the way it responds to you. The way my breath catches sometimes when I see you, the way a shiver runs along my arm when you touch me, or the way my heart beats, sometimes in my throat or my ears when you kiss me. I'm not afraid of feeling those…those physical reactions anymore. And I'm not afraid of giving up control the way I have to give up control to a seizure."

She'd hiked herself up on an elbow, her eyes full of emotion and wonder. "When…when you make love to me, it's…it's like I fly, Lee. I've always been so afraid of being out of control. But with you…it's so wonderful. It's so wonderful to let go."

He'd felt the sting behind his eyes and hadn't even tried to deny the cause.

"You're wonderful," he'd whispered. "And so very brave."

"I'm not brave."

But she was. She'd grown into a woman who had yet to realize her own strengths.

He hadn't told her that. She wouldn't want to believe it, anyway. Just as he hadn't told her that he loved her. Because for him, it was still hard to believe he had the capability. Ellie had moved past her fears, but he was still struggling. If he tried not to be aware, if he tried not to overthink it, maybe, just maybe, it would happen without him spoiling the best thing that had ever happened to him.

So, no. He hadn't told her he loved her. He'd shown her instead. With soul-deep kisses and the most gentle kind of love that he knew how to give, he'd taken her to that place where she could fly and not be afraid of the fall.

That had been last night. Just last night.

In the rocker in the corner of the bedroom, he looked from his tightly clasped hands to the woman, pale and exhausted, in the bed. He hadn't been there to catch her this time. The helplessness of it ate at him.

And no, he'd never understood fear.

Not the way he understood it now.

Ellie opened her eyes slowly. The sense of lethargy, the lingering headache, the dead weight of her legs and arms—they were all too familiar to her.

It took only a few moments to understand what had happened, but as usual after a seizure, what she didn't know was when. When did it happen? Where had she been? What had she done? How had she gotten into bed?

She looked around her room, willed the clock on her bedside table into focus—11:52. Almost midnight. Almost midnight of what day? How many had she lost?

"Hi," a gruff voice said from across the room.

She turned her head and saw Lee sitting in her rocker. His face looked haggard in the pale light that leaked in from the hall. His eyes looked weary.

"Hi," she whispered. She hadn't wanted him to ever see her this way, even though she'd known it had been inevitable that he would. It still didn't make it any easier to face him, to wonder what he'd seen and how he'd reacted. Had she done something horribly embarrassing? Had it repulsed him?

She heard him cross the room. Felt his weight as he eased a hip onto the mattress.

"How are you feeling?"

Lost. Embarrassed. Angry. Confused. "Fine. I'm feeling fine."

He touched a hand to her hair. "And I'm Martha

Stewart, but, hey, if you believe me, I'll believe you. So…should we move on to the weather?''

She smiled. He made it so easy to smile. "Dark. The weather forecast is dark.''

He smiled too. "Well, that's a relief. Now I can plan my night.''

She snaked her hand out from under the covers. He took it in both of his, brought it to his lips.

The breath he let out wasn't at all steady. She understood then how upset he was. "I'm sorry—''

"Don't. Don't even think it. You have nothing to be sorry for.''

But she did. She was sorry this was a part of her. His silence said he was sorry, too.

"Do you need to get up?'' he asked gruffly. "Use the bathroom? Are you hungry?''

She shook her head on both counts.

He watched her face. "Want some company in there?''

A wave of tenderness, of gratefulness, of love washed through her. All she could do was nod.

He was out of his clothes and burrowed next to her so fast she was hardly aware that he'd moved.

"Wow,'' she said when he'd wrapped himself around her and surrounded her with his heat.

"Yeah,'' he said, snuggling close. "Wow.''

"You make everything good,'' she said against his throat, and felt his lifeblood beating there.

"You *are* everything good.'' He pressed a kiss to her hair.

And, wrapped in his arms, she fell asleep, less diminished and, because of his total acceptance, far more complete.

* * *

It was hard to listen to him tell her about it. But the next morning, feeling much better though not fully recovered, she asked him to tell her what her parents never would.

"What happened to me? What did I do?"

He sat with her at the table, where the morning sun cut prisms through the ancient leaded-glass window, and told her what she wanted to know.

He held her hands while he talked, slowly rubbing his thumb over the backs of her knuckles, his gaze drifting from there to her face and down again.

When he finished, she sat back with a bewildered sigh. "That's it?"

He shrugged. "That's everything."

He rose, refilled his coffee mug then poured her more tea.

She was quiet for a long moment, digesting all he had told her. No, it hadn't been pretty and, yes, it was difficult to hear, but it was also as if this huge black hole that was a part of her wasn't as huge and as black as it had been.

"You know those scary movies," she began thoughtfully, "the ones where all through the movie you want to hide your eyes behind your hands because you don't know what monster is going to jump out at you from the dark?"

His gaze was intent on hers as he sat back down at the kitchen table. "I don't hide behind my hands. Ever."

She smiled. At the wonderful way he had of giving import to what she was saying, yet turning a potentially dark conversation back toward the light.

"Okay. So a big, brave, macho guy like you doesn't hide behind his hands. But for a scaredy-cat like me who does, I'm terrified for the first three-fourths of the movie and then, when the monster finally makes his appearance, it's really not so scary anymore. It was the unknown that was frightening. It's still the unknown," she added softly.

She ran a thumb over the rim of her cup, thought for another long moment—thought of all her parents had given her and of this one thing they had withheld. "I wonder why they would never tell me."

"Maybe they thought it would upset you."

"Not knowing upset me. Imagining the awful things I could have done upset me. But now I know and it…it sounds pretty…I don't know…uneventful, really."

"If you don't count the fact that you scared ten years off my life."

Again she smiled. "Ten years? Hmm. Good thing I'm a sucker for older men."

He snagged her wrist, pulled her carefully onto his lap. Kissed her with feeling. "Damn good thing."

A couple of days later, when Lee mentioned his plan for a honeymoon and had asked Ellie to think of a spot she'd like to go, she'd been thinking Bozeman. Maybe Denver. He'd been thinking bigger, and a week later he delivered. He took her to New York City.

They'd explored MOMA and the Frick. He'd taken her to Chinatown and Union Square, to Tavern on the Green and *Phantom of the Opera.* She'd cried at Ellis Island—"for those poor desperate souls"—and lost her breath at the top of the Empire State Building, gaped at the opulent extravagance of tea at the Plaza Hotel and the elegance of a candlelit dinner at the Rainbow Room.

And now they stood in the middle of Times Square with life and noise and excitement teeming around them like a wild carnival ride. It was their last night here. It was midnight and she was glowing. Tomorrow he would take her home. But first she wanted a midnight carriage ride around Central Park.

"He's from Dublin," she whispered dreamily as they clip-clopped by Rockefeller Center and moved on toward St. Patrick's Cathedral. "Imagine that. Our carriage driver is from Dublin."

Everything was a wonder to her. It showed in her eyes as she settled back and smiled, looking for all the world like Cinderella in her pumpkin coach, the night of the ball.

He'd have given her a castle if he could have worked out a deal. He'd have given her anything. And as soon as they returned to Shiloh, he did what he could to lay the world at her feet—at least a new world for her.

"But I don't know anything about computers," she said, when he'd finished setting up a new desktop model in her father's den.

"You don't have to know much more than this."

He showed her how to boot up and how to log on to the Net. Then he gave her the address of a Web site dedicated to epilepsy.

"I didn't know," she said, when he found her still in front of the monitor almost six hours later. "I didn't have any idea."

"And now you do," he said gently.

The site was one of many that linked to others, where not only medical facts but also personal stories were posted and shared.

She rose from her chair, tears in her eyes, and

threw her arms around his neck. "Oh, Lee. I feel like I know these people. I know what they feel. I live what they live. Thank you. I...I don't even know how to explain how this makes me feel."

She wiped her eyes with the back of her hand, smiling and crying and laughing all at the same time. "It's one thing to know you are one of many, but...it's not the same as actually reading someone else's story and knowing that they've been where you've been. It's...it's the difference between looking at a pie chart and eating a piece of pie," she exclaimed with a huge grin. "It gives it texture and flavor and heart."

He looked into her smiling eyes and didn't think he'd ever known anyone with more heart than she had.

"Now tell me," she demanded, and bounced back to the keyboard. "Tell me how I can talk to them."

"Tomorrow," he insisted with a laugh, and tugged her into his arms. "Tomorrow will be soon enough. I've got something else in mind for you tonight."

Ellie had never been happier in her life. She felt as if she was bouncing around in a magic bubble, insulated from old memories and past hurts. It seemed too good to be real, too sweet to be true. And then it just got better.

"Classes?" she said, when Lee came home from a trip to Bozeman one night and tossed some brochures from the community college onto the kitchen table. "What kind of classes?"

"Take your pick." He dug around for a course catalog and handed it to her. "I thought we could both take one. I could use a refresher on Excel for some spreadsheets I want to work up on the breeding program. You could take anything you like. Something on creative writing, maybe? Poetry? They have gardening classes and some art classes. Even a class on building a Web site.''

She launched herself into his arms. Kissed him long and deep.

''What?'' he asked, grinning because she was so happy.

''You.''

''Okay.'' He sat down on a kitchen chair and lifted her onto his lap so she was straddling him. ''I'll bite. Me what?''

''You are a wonderful man.''

''Because I brought you some course catalogs?''

''Because—'' she started unbuttoning his shirt ''—because I love the idea of going to school.'' She peeled the shirt back from his chest, nibbled on a spot just below his collarbone. ''And because I love you,'' she added shyly.

When he only smiled, she started unbuttoning her own shirt. ''And because you like page fifty-three as much as I do.''

He let out a whoop of laughter. ''*You* are an insatiable little wanton.''

She bounced off his lap and headed for the stairs at a run. ''Page fifty-three,'' she reminded him with a huge grin.

He was right behind her. ''I'm too old for this.''

It was her turn to laugh. ''Come on, *old man*. I promise, I'll go easy on you.''

''The hell you will,'' he growled, and catching her on the third step, tossed her over his shoulder and took the rest of the stairs two at a time.

Ten

Lee gathered the spread sheet he'd been working on and zipped it into his briefcase. Then he slipped out of the classroom and headed across the hall to wait for Ellie's class to let out.

They'd been making the trip to Bozeman for night classes twice a week for a little over a month now. It hadn't taken but one class and he'd started struggling with some truths that had been easy to dismiss—or at least ignore—while the two of them had been fairly well isolated at Shiloh. Truths he couldn't ignore any longer.

Old man.

She'd kidded him about being an old man on more than one occasion. Her teasing words had banged around in his head more and more often as the days went by—and now the joke wasn't so funny. In fact, it was giving him a headache.

Okay, so he may not be an old man, but Ellie was definitely a young woman—a fact that he'd never been more aware of since seeing her in a college setting.

She was nineteen, for Pete's sake, and she should have been given the chance to experience some of the things nineteen-year-olds are supposed to experience.

Old man.

He'd been fooling himself. All along he'd been fooling himself into believing that he done her a favor by marrying her.

His expression grim, he looked through the textured-glass windowpane of her classroom door. She didn't know he was there. Neither did the young stud putting on the moves, when Ellie laughed at something he said and smiled prettily up at him.

The kid had the build of an athlete and the look of a ladies' man, and Lee should be used to his—and every other man's—reaction to her. She turned heads no matter where she went, and these college guys were perpetually on the make.

He looked the younger man over and couldn't shrug off the twinge of envy he'd tried to deny during the past couple of months. This guy was heartbreak material—even Lee could see that. He oozed confidence and charm and had a smile that no doubt had every coed within grinning distance drooling on their keyboards.

He couldn't have been more than twenty. Just as he couldn't have known that he wouldn't live to see twenty-one if he didn't back away from his wife.

Lee shoved open the door.

"Lee." Ellie's smile grew wider when she saw him. "We're just about done here but come look—

look what John showed me. John, this is my husband,
Lee Savage.''

John should have had the sense to go about three
shades of pale and the presence of mind to back off.
When he did neither, but sized Lee up with a long,
assessing once-over instead, Lee placed a hand on
Ellie's shoulder.

It was sophomoric and proprietary, not to mention
possessive and defensive, and there hadn't been a
damn thing he could do to stop himself. Ellie was
oblivious to his ridiculous show of staking a claim.

John, with a pointed look at Lee's hand, gave a
small but reluctant nod of concession.

''Savage,'' he said, and with a murmured goodbye
to Ellie, strolled back to his computer.

All the way home Lee had brooded about how he'd
reacted, what he'd done, how it had made him feel.
Most of all, though, he brooded about those truths that
wouldn't go away.

When he'd returned to Shiloh, it had been with the
conviction that Ellie had needed him to take care of
her. It was obvious now, that all she'd ever needed
was the chance to find out who she was and what she
wanted. She hadn't needed him for that.

In fact, it was becoming more and more apparent
that she really hadn't needed him for much of anything.

Their classes ended mid-June, and Ellie was anxious to go to work setting up her own Web page.

''I have so many plans,'' she told John on the last
day of class. ''So many people I want to reach, so
many invitations I want to extend to anyone and
everyone who doesn't understand…who might feel as

alone as I did and who just need a chance to share what they've been through.''

Aside from her plans for the Web page, one of the most wonderful things to have come out of her class was her friendship with John Tyler. When she'd encountered him that first session, she'd been a little nervous about having to see him on a regular basis. But they'd both grown up a lot since those hurtful years when he'd been, in his words, ''a Neanderthal idiot'' and she'd been, in her words, ''a poor pitiful Pearl.'' All those years that she'd harbored resentment toward him he'd been hating himself and trying to figure out some way to break through the stone wall she'd erected.

Well, they were friends now. They even shared a little bit of a history, and she was glad he'd made that first overture of peace. Now that class was over, she missed talking to him.

And as the days passed and she worked on her Web page, she also missed Lee. She tried to ignore the unsettling feeling that something was very wrong between them. She told herself that the reason he was a little quiet lately, the reason he seemed to be working outside longer, staying up later, was because he was busy, too. And because he was giving her room and time to work on her project.

Life was good. Life was very good. She had a new friend in John, and she and Peg made it a point to have lunch together at least once a week. She wasn't going to let her insecurities, her niggling little suspicion that suggested Lee was pulling away from her, interrupt it.

It was only her imagination that something was out of place when he seemed sort of thoughtful or preoccupied. Didn't he still make love to her with a tenderness that made her weep? She was just imagining that there was desperation when he kissed her—even though she couldn't stop wondering and worrying about what was going on in his mind.

Ellie heard the truck pull up one Saturday morning and walked out onto the front porch. When she saw who it was, she bounced down the steps to greet him and was promptly wrapped in strong arms, swung around in a circle, and given a big smacking kiss on the cheek.

"John Tyler," she gasped, laughing up at him as he held her and grinned his poster boy grin, "a simple hello would have done just fine."

"But this way is so much more fun."

She laughed again. "Well put me down. I can't breathe, for heaven's sake."

"Ellie, sweet thing, you've stolen my breath for so many years now, it only seems fair that I steal a little bit of yours."

"Is that what you've got on your mind, Tyler? Stealing?"

Ellie looked over her shoulder to see Lee standing behind them, his face grim, his voice as hard as the hammer he held in his hand that he'd been using to rebuild a box stall.

"Hello, Savage," John said, slowly letting Ellie go with an affectionate squeeze and another quick grin. "How's it shakin'?"

"It's shakin' just fine," Lee said in a steely voice that made Ellie frown and wonder about the heat in his eyes and his rigid stance.

"So…" Lee slung his weight onto one foot and

crossed his arms over his chest. "You were in the neighborhood or what?"

Since Shiloh was nowhere near anyone's neighborhood, Ellie thought Lee's question a little odd, but she was so happy to see John that she let it roll on by.

"What *are* you doing way out here?" she asked, then remembered her manners. "Oh, wait. I don't get to play hostess very often. Come on up to the house. I'll get us all something to drink, then we can talk."

She was halfway up the steps before she realized the men were still planted where they stood.

"Are you coming?" she asked, puzzled by John's grin, which could only be described as challenging, and Lee's scowl, which was flat-out fierce.

"In a minute," Lee said, his eyes never leaving John's face. "You go on, Ellie. I want to show John the box stall—maybe get his take on a couple of things."

When she hesitated, unsure, John's grin just widened. "Give us five and we'll be there."

Then the two of them turned and headed for the barn, leaving Ellie with the distinct impression that there was much more to their conversation than box stalls.

Lee was steaming. Because Ellie was beaming at John-boy here, who didn't have the wherewithal to comprehend that he was about a hammer handle away from losing a few of the pearly whites that made his lady-killer grin so irresistible.

"You can't get your own woman, Tyler? You've got to come out here sniffing after mine?"

"Is that what she is? Yours? As in property?" John

asked, his smile gone, his expression leaning toward combative.

Lee stared at the young man long and hard, then purposefully dropped the hammer so he wouldn't be tempted to use it. "You want to explain to me where you get off, coming to *my* home, kissing *my* wife and asking me a question like that?"

Tyler didn't have anything to say for a long moment. When he finally spoke, Lee figured the kid couldn't possibly know what kind of risk he was taking. "A long time ago I did a lousy thing to Ellie. I hurt her. Worse, I let her be hurt. I was a kid then. And I was stupid. I'm not a kid anymore," he added, just a hint of a threat in his voice. "And I don't figure that it would be right if I stood by and watched her get hurt again."

"And you figure I'm going to hurt her," Lee said, more statement than question.

"I guess that's what I came here to find out."

The anger came from deep inside. So deep he hadn't known it was there. So fierce he wasn't sure what kept him from laying John Tyler and his White-Knight attitude lower than barn dirt. "And I guess that still leaves me wondering why you think you have the right."

Something flickered in John's eyes. "Oh, no. No, man," he said, patting the air between them as if to ward off the thought. "It's nothing like that. Hell, I've never had a chance with Ellie. Not that way. Not when we were kids…not now. And even if she was interested—which she absolutely is not," he added with emphasis, "I'd never graze in another man's pasture, if you know what I mean."

"Then your point is?" Lee ground out.

"My point is, she is nuts about you. I just want to make sure the feeling's mutual."

The silence that settled would have made a lesser man head for the nearest exit. At a run. John Tyler, for all his coverboy looks, was not a lesser man. Either that or he had a death wish.

"Shiloh," John said, holding his ground. "It's a pretty high-ticket piece of property."

"Ah. So it's the profit margin you figure I'm working toward," Lee said, understanding where this was headed.

"It's crossed my mind. Quite a bit, in fact, until I ran into Ellie again at those night classes."

"And?"

"And I'd never seen her so confident. Or so happy."

Quiet filled the barn like the daylight that crept in through the door when Ellie opened it and called out to them.

They remained locked in combative silence until John broke it. "So, I came out here to make sure I was reading the situation right."

"Overlooking the fact that it's none of your business…what's your read now?"

John grinned. "It's a good read. And you're good for her. So…congratulations on your marriage. You're a lucky man."

He sobered then, looked Lee straight in the eye. "Keep her happy. She deserves to be happy. And now that I've seen for myself that you're ready to knock the block off any fool stupid enough to question your good intentions," he added, tongue in cheek, and with a quick glance at the hammer lying by Lee's feet, "I think maybe you just might be good enough for her."

Ellie had crossed the barn and had tucked herself along Lee's side before he could manage to do anything but shake his head and give up a halfhearted smile when John shot another flirting grin at his wife and invited himself up to the house for a cold one.

As Ellie stood at the kitchen sink finishing up dishes that night, she decided that she would never understand men. True, she'd had limited experience dealing with them, but the experience she'd had, well, it was baffling. Take this afternoon with John and Lee. She could have sworn that when she went looking for them in the barn she was going to find one or both of them covered with blood—though she didn't have a clue what they'd been angry about.

Instead, they were actually laughing at each other's stupid jokes by the time John had left after a supper that she hadn't had to work too hard at talking him into staying for.

Lee...Lee was still something of a puzzle. After John left, he'd withdrawn again. She was ready to admit that he'd started pulling away from her about the time they'd started taking those classes. She'd sensed then that he'd been struggling with something. She'd seen the look on his face whenever he'd come into her class to pick her up.

Sometimes he'd actually looked angry. No. It had been less than anger. It had been something else...something she had never been able to figure out. Something that had haunted her—and evidently haunted him, too.

On a deep sigh she looked hard at the picture she'd

propped on the kitchen windowsill and dried her hands on a dish towel. She'd found it when she'd been cleaning the roll-top desk this morning. It was a picture of Lee when he'd first come to Shiloh, before she'd ever been born. The look on his face—as he'd stood there by her daddy's side—made her heart break. It was a look full of hurt and distrust and defiant pride. Her daddy's hand had been on his shoulder, his touch an extension of his love, an overture of trust, a welcome that the ten-year-old boy Lee had been had only to reach out and take to his heart—yet Lee had looked as alone as she felt without him.

He looked, she realized, with tears misting her eyes, as he had looked so often during the past few weeks. Distrustful, confused. Alone.

Her heart tripped. Her breath quickened. She stared at the picture of that lost little boy who had come to Shiloh broken and abused. And with the wisdom of a woman in love, she finally understood. So many things.

"Oh, Lee," she whispered, taking the picture in her hand. Running her thumb over that beautiful, unsmiling, defiant face, she finally understood that of the two of them he was still the most wounded.

She went to him at dusk that night. In her flowing white gown, with the wind whipping her hair, she went out on the porch where he sat in brooding silence.

"Go inside, Ellie," he said after a long moment. "It's too cool out here tonight."

She wasn't going anywhere. Not without him. Not ever again.

"It's colder in there. Without you."

She moved to kneel at his feet, watched the turmoil in his eyes and knew she'd been right to come to him. As she'd once before come to him, a woman determined to love her man.

Then she eased up onto his lap until he was forced to put his arms around her or let her tumble to the cold porch floor. It took no leap of faith to know he'd never let her fall.

He let out a deep breath, then surrendered and, pulling her to him, buried his face in her hair.

She hugged him to her breast, loving the feel of his hair beneath her hands, the heat of his big, strong body surrounding her.

"I love you, Lee."

His breath came out on a long and ragged shudder. He stared at her face, ran his thumb along her cheek. "You could have been anything. Anything you wanted to be."

Her heart broke as the complexities of this man's soul started to unravel around them. "That's what's been eating at you lately? You think you've taken something away from me?"

He looked away, and her heart stuttered for several beats. "Are you sorry you married me?"

He held her hard against him. "I'm sorry that I took away your choices."

"Listen to me," she said after a long breath. Framing his face in her hands, she made him look into her eyes. "Everything I am, everything I need, is right here with you. I know my own mind, Lee, and it has always been with you. Always.

"No," she insisted when he shook his head. "Just listen. For too long, I let something I couldn't control, control me. Who I was, what I did, what I thought of myself. You've opened up my world. *You,* Lee. You have shown me who I am. And the only choices I've ever had—you have given to me. Choices, Lee. About that, you're right. It's all about choices. Now please…please trust me to make them.''

She caressed his face, looked deep in his eyes. ''I choose Shiloh. I choose you.''

Lee stared at this woman who was his wife. He listened to her words, heard the strength in them, saw the conviction in her eyes, felt the love that spilled out from her heart. She believed. She believed every word she said, that he had given her choices, not taken them away. That she was strong, not in spite of him but because of what she was and what they were together.

She believed. In them. In him. And in that moment, she finally made him a believer, too. Right or wrong, deserved or not, he was going to hold on to the belief—just as he was going to hold on to her and in the process give her the gift of every opportunity she had ever missed.

''Well,'' he whispered, folding her against him, feeling the heart that she had given him so freely beat, steady and strong and true. ''You may have had choices but I never have. Never. Not when it comes to you.''

Midnight was soft, and securely wrapped around the bed in the room with pink flowers on the wall. Shiloh slept even as husband and wife lay awake.

''I want to have your baby,'' Ellie whispered into the quiet.

As happy as he was in this moment, he felt his body tense involuntarily. He'd been waiting for this.

Dreading this. Wrestling with what he would say when she asked.

"Give me some time," he said into the dark. "Give me some time to get used to the idea."

In the moonlight he saw her eyes mist over with tears. He brushed the back of a knuckle across her petal-soft cheek. "And then we'll talk to Doc, okay? Just talk," he insisted, then banded his arms around her. "As much as I'd love to give you a baby…it tears me up to think of you taking that kind of risk."

She kissed him gently. "Life is a risk. The sweetest kind…. When you're ready," she murmured, settling back down in his arms, "only when you're ready, we'll talk with Doc. Then we'll make the decision together."

He was quiet for a long moment, aching for her and the disappointment that their decision might bring her. "And what if the decision is no? What if it's not safe for you to have babies?"

She was quiet, too, dealing with the possibility, mourning the potential loss. "Shiloh has a lot to offer a child," she said at last, her eyes like velvet mist in the night. "Especially a child who has never been offered much of a chance."

A child like he had been. A child who had grown into a man who had thought the exceptional woman in his arms had needed mending. Instead he'd been the one who'd been broken—and she had mended him.

So much warmth, so much wisdom, so much love. He hung on to it. He hung on to her. As he was going to hang on to her for the rest of his life.

"I love you, Ellie."

"I know," she whispered softly. "I think I've always known."

He showed her with his touch then, with the deep glide and penetration of his body, what he couldn't hope to accomplish with mere words.

He took her up, he took her over, to that place where they could both soar free, to that place where she was woman-strong and he was the best man he could ever be…and where neither one of them had to be afraid of the fall.

* * * * *

Feel like a star with Silhouette.

We will fly you and a guest to New York City for an exciting weekend stay at a glamorous 5-star hotel. Experience a refreshing day at one of New York's trendiest spas and have your photo taken by a professional. Plus, receive $1,000 U.S. spending money!

Flowers…long walks…dinner for two… how does Silhouette Books make romance come alive for you?

Send us a script, with 500 words or less, along with visuals (only drawings, magazine cutouts or photographs or combination thereof). Show us how Silhouette Makes Your Love Come Alive. Be creative and have fun. No purchase necessary. All entries must be clearly marked with your name, address and telephone number. All entries will become property of Silhouette and are not returnable. **Contest closes September 28, 2001.**

Please send your entry to: **Silhouette Makes You a Star!**

In U.S.A.	In Canada
P.O. Box 9069	P.O. Box 637
Buffalo, NY, 14269-9069	Fort Erie, ON, L2A 5X3

Look for contest details on the next page, by visiting www.eHarlequin.com or request a copy by sending a self-addressed envelope to the applicable address above. Contest open to Canadian and U.S. residents who are 18 or over. Void where prohibited.

Where love comes alive™

Our lucky winner's photo will appear in a Silhouette ad. Join the fun!

SRMYAS1

HARLEQUIN "SILHOUETTE MAKES YOU A STAR!" CONTEST 1308
OFFICIAL RULES
NO PURCHASE NECESSARY TO ENTER

1. To enter, follow directions published in the offer to which you are responding. Contest begins June 1, 2001, and ends on September 28, 2001. Entries must be postmarked by September 28, 2001, and received by October 5, 2001. Enter by hand-printing (or typing) on an 8 ½" x 11" piece of paper your name, address (including zip code), contest number/name and attaching a script containing 500 words or less, along with drawings, photographs or magazine cutouts, or combinations thereof (i.e., collage) on no larger than 9" x 12" piece of paper, describing how the Silhouette books make romance come alive for you. Mail via first-class mail to: Harlequin "Silhouette Makes You a Star!" Contest 1308, (in the U.S.) P.O. Box 9069, Buffalo, NY 14269-9069, (in Canada) P.O. Box 637, Fort Erie, Ontario, Canada L2A 5X3. Limit one entry per person, household or organization.

2. Contests will be judged by a panel of members of the Harlequin editorial, marketing and public relations staff. Fifty percent of criteria will be judged against script and fifty percent will be judged against drawing, photographs and/or magazine cutouts. Judging criteria will be based on the following:

    * Sincerity—25%
    * Originality and Creativity—50%
    * Emotionally Compelling—25%

    In the event of a tie, duplicate prizes will be awarded. Decisions of the judges are final.

3. All entries become the property of Torstar Corp. and may be used for future promotional purposes. Entries will not be returned. No responsibility is assumed for lost, late, illegible, incomplete, inaccurate, nondelivered or misdirected mail.

4. Contest open only to residents of the U.S. (except Puerto Rico) and Canada who are 18 years of age or older, and is void wherever prohibited by law; all applicable laws and regulations apply. Any litigation within the Province of Quebec respecting the conduct or organization of a publicity contest may be submitted to the Régie des alcools, des courses et des jeux for a ruling. Any litigation respecting the awarding of a prize may be submitted to the Régie des alcools, des courses et des jeux only for the purpose of helping the parties reach a settlement. Employees and immediate family members of Torstar Corp. and D. L. Blair, Inc., their affiliates, subsidiaries and all other agencies, entities and persons connected with the use, marketing or conduct of this contest are not eligible to enter. Taxes on prizes are the sole responsibility of the winner. Acceptance of any prize offered constitutes permission to use winner's name, photograph or other likeness for the purposes of advertising, trade and promotion on behalf of Torstar Corp., its affiliates and subsidiaries without further compensation to the winner, unless prohibited by law.

5. Winner will be determined no later than November 30, 2001, and will be notified by mail. Winner will be required to sign and return an Affidavit of Eligibility/Release of Liability/Publicity Release form within 15 days after winner notification. Noncompliance within that time period may result in disqualification and an alternative winner may be selected. All travelers must execute a Release of Liability prior to ticketing and must possess required travel documents (e.g., passport, photo ID) where applicable. Trip must be booked by December 31, 2001, and completed within one year of notification. No substitution of prize permitted by winner. Torstar Corp. and D. L. Blair, Inc., their parents, affiliates and subsidiaries are not responsible for errors in printing of contest, entries and/or game pieces. In the event of printing or other errors that may result in unintended prize values or duplication of prizes, all affected game pieces or entries shall be null and void. **Purchase or acceptance of a product offer does not improve your chances of winning.**

6. Prizes: (1) Grand Prize—A 2-night/3-day trip for two (2) to New York City, including round-trip coach air transportation nearest winner's home and hotel accommodations (double occupancy) at The Plaza Hotel, a glamorous afternoon makeover at a trendy New York spa, $1,000 in U.S. spending money and an opportunity to have a professional photo taken and appear in a Silhouette advertisement (approximate retail value: $7,000). (10) Ten Runner-Up Prizes of gift packages (retail value $50 ea.). Prizes consist of only those items listed as part of the prize. Limit one prize per person. Prize is valued in U.S. currency.

7. For the name of the winner (available after December 31, 2001) send a self-addressed, stamped envelope to: Harlequin "Silhouette Makes You a Star!" Contest 1197 Winners, P.O. Box 4200 Blair, NE 68009-4200 or you may access the www.eHarlequin.com Web site through February 28, 2002.

Contest sponsored by Torstar Corp., P.O Box 9042, Buffalo, NY 14269-9042.

SRMYAS2

If you enjoyed what you just read,
then we've got an offer you can't resist!

Take 2 bestselling love stories FREE!

Plus get a FREE surprise gift!